Manufactured in the United States

Illustrations by Cameron Wilson for Soulsimplicity Design and Publishing.

TITAN WARRIORS
ALIGNMENT OF POWER

BY KARLTON T. CLAY
ILLUSTRATED BY CAMERON WILSON

EDITED BY
KARMEN SCOTT
CARLYN G. MORRIS
BARBARA BUDNICK

TITAN WARRIORS
ALIGNMENT OF POWER

TABLE OF CONTENTS

I dedicate this book to all of the young people and the young at heart with big imaginations.

Continue to dream big and reach for the stars.

And to young Karlton, who wrote all of those stories after you finished bouncing the ball at your grandparents' house, your aunts' house, and at home...
Keep going.

I hope that I'm making you proud.

PROLOGUE

THOUSANDS OF LIGHT-YEARS AWAY FROM PLANET EARTH

I gotta get out here. I have to get them to safety. The future depends on it.

Those words echoed over and over in his head in between his scattered breathing and the thumping of his heart beating out of his chest. Brodus continued to run frantically through the woods with tree limbs and leaves whacking him in the face at every turn. Even though every muscle inside of his body wanted to stop to rest, the sounds of evil behind him forced him to continue on this journey.

I gotta get out here. I have to get them to safety. The future depends on it.

Brodus felt that his legs were beginning to ache the more he ran. With every breath, the tighter his hand became as several glimmers of light began to shine in the palms of his hands. Brodus could hear the sound of hooves galloping, getting closer and closer, but he knew that he could not give up. He had to complete his mission.

I gotta get out here. I have to get them to safety. The future depends on it.

Brodus remained persistent in his voyage to escape the darkness and evil that was making its way towards him. He looked up smiling as if he began to see the light at the end of the tunnel. But suddenly, Brodus could feel his feet ram into a very large object as he lost his balance and fell flat on the ground hitting his face on a large rock. Feeling the pain, Brodus rolled over in pain and agony realizing that he had tripped over a huge tree branch that appeared to be strategically placed on the ground.

As he wiped his face realizing that blood was trickling down from the top of his head like a flowing river, an evil force began to overshadow Brodus. He knew what time it was. He knew what his fate would entail as he opened his eyes to several horsemen sitting on their steed. Each horse had silky hair that was as dark as the night sky and fiery eyes that burned like the pits of eternal damnation.

Suddenly, the biggest, scariest, darkest force of evil rode up to the front of the herd on his stallion. This ominous, dark creature was huge in stature with his body covered entirely in black armor, his head and face covered with a black helmet, and a large black sword dangling from his side. Brodus looked at the evil that surrounded him in fear as the vile creature's stallion sniffed heavily on Brodus' clothes.

I gotta get out here. I have to get them to safety. The future depends on it.

Those words continued to flow through Brodus' mind as the dark creature leaped off his horse making a huge thud as he landed on the ground feet first. He stood over Brodus. Brodus looked at him with terror in his eyes, but he held tight to the source of life that was in his hand. Suddenly, the evil monstrosity reached out and grabbed Brodus by the throat completely lifting him off the ground. Brodus continued to hold steadfast even though he could feel the oxygen slowly leaving his lungs as he began to gasp for air.

"Give me the crosses!" the evil behemoth snarled.

"No, Nefarious, I will not."

"You dare to defy me! Give me those crosses now, Old Man!"

Brodus did not respond. Brodus tried to steal any second to take a breath, but he could feel that the next second may be his last.

"If you value your life, you will give them to me," Nefarious threatened.

"To live... is to Christ..." Brodus replied barely. "And to die... is to gain."

"My patience has ended with you!" Nefarious shouted as his grip around Brodus' throat tightened. "Give them to me now!"

Brodus could barely hold on, but he knew what he had to do. He had a mission, and it was his purpose to complete it – by any means necessary. "Okay... I'll... I'll… give them to you," he lightly said.

Immediately, Nefarious released his grip on Brodus' throat, and Brodus fell to the ground. Nefarious and the other horsemen cackled as Brodus struggled to regain his composure. After a few seconds, Brodus stood tall, and suddenly, the light began to glimmer from his palm as he opened his hand revealing six small crosses on golden chains wrapped in a papyrus. Each cross glowed in a different color: gold, silver, bronze, blue, purple, and scarlet.

Nefarious looked at Brodus and snarled. Brodus was not sure what would happen next, but he knew that the time had come for him to complete his journey. Brodus reached out towards Nefarious with the crosses in his hand. Nefarious and the other horsemen began to grow intrigued and excited as the light made its way closer and closer towards them. Nefarious began to reach his hand out towards the crosses, but suddenly, with all his might, Brodus slung the crosses into the atmosphere. The crosses continued to shine brightly until they disappeared into the night sky as if to become a part of the distant stars.

"You fool!" Nefarious screamed.

Nefarious instantaneously grabbed Brodus' throat in the same exact spot that he had before, but this time was a lot tighter than the last. Brodus' gasps for air became harder and more frequent as Nefarious' grip grew tighter and tighter.

"May… God… have… mercy… on… your soul," Brodus cried out.

"Lucky for me," Nefarious snarled, "I HAVE NO SOUL!"

Suddenly, a loud crack was heard that echoed throughout the woods as Brodus' body went limp in

Nefarious' hand and the old papyrus fell from Brodus' hand and to the ground. Nefarious snarled as he looked at Brodus' dead body with hate. The other horsemen stood at attention awaiting their next move as they watched Nefarious throw Brodus' body forcefully to the ground. The wind began to blow as the leaves twirled across Nefarious' foot. He looked down seeing the papyrus that was once held tightly in Brodus' hand. Intrigued by what had come across his path, Nefarious knelt and picked it up. He opened the papyrus and as he began to read, the anger that filled his empty heart vigorously grew.

"Let no man despise their youth," Nefarious read, "for they are examples of love, righteousness, faith, and truth. This prophesy will fulfill, and the Lord picks. The keepers of the crosses are youth of six. The revelation at the eleventh hour will be the holders of the alignment of power."

Nefarious growled angrily as he tore the old papyrus into small pieces. Suddenly, the wind once again blew across the ground carrying the small pieces of the old papyrus away.

"I will get those crosses," Nefarious snarled. "Even if it takes… FOREVER!"

The horsemen bowed down on their horses as Nefarious' growl grew more powerful. Nefarious turned to look to his servants, and they could see the bright red, evil glare in his eyes. Then, he looked up to the sky and noticed a faint view of what appeared to be planet Earth.

CHAPTER ONE

GARDEN CITY, GEORGIA

PRESENT DAY

I can't believe that I have to do this.

Fifteen-year-old Jared Taylor looked at himself in the mirror. He sighed in despair realizing that today would be his first day at a brand-new school in a brand-new city. He walked over to his bed and sat down. He looked over on the side of his bed and looked at a picture of him and his friends from the sunny city of Los Angeles, California. He picked up the picture frame and looked at his face. He looked as if he was so happy and so content with life. However, he sighed again realizing that life was never going to be the same.

"Boys! Come on downstairs for breakfast!" he could hear his dad calling from downstairs.

"This is going to suck," Jared sulked as he placed the picture frame back on his side table.

Jared picked up his bookbag and sadly walked out of his bedroom understanding that this was officially the first day of the rest of his "new" life.

As Jared made his way towards the staircase, he could hear another door closing. He looked to see his brother, Myles, who was two years older than him, happily walking up to him.

"Shake a leg, little brother. It's the beginning of the rest of our lives," Myles excitedly said as he walked down the stairs.

Jared rolled his eyes as he followed behind his brother.

Myles rushed into the dining room, and he saw his father sitting at the head of the table reading the morning paper. "Good morning, Dad!"

"Good morning, Myles!" Mr. Taylor responded as he closed his newspaper and placed it down on the table.

While Myles sat down at the table and poured himself some orange juice, Jared slowly walked in and plopped down in the chair next to Myles. Mr. Taylor could see the sullen look on his younger son's face.

"Good morning, Jared," Mr. Taylor said.

"Morning," Jared grimly replied.

"Son, what's the matter with you?"

"Nothing," Jared responded knowing that he needed to watch his tone when it came to talking to his father.

"Good, then, act like it," Mr. Taylor sternly said. "You woke up this morning in your right mind. You got activity in your limbs. Be happy about that."

"Yeah. Like me!" Myles happily added smiling at his little brother.

Jared sarcastically smiled back at Myles. He did not ask for a sermon from his father or a suck-up response from his overtly optimistic older brother. But Jared knew how to pick his battles, and this one was definitely not a fight that he wanted to endure especially with the battle that could possibly ensue on the first day of his new school.

While Jared sat quietly stewing in his thoughts, the smell of bacon and eggs began to fill the room. Jared looked up to see his mother carrying two plates of bacon and eggs.

"Good morning, Myles," Mrs. Taylor greeted as she placed the plates in front of her growing boys. "And good morning, Jared."

"Good morning, Ma!" Myles exclaimed.

"Morning, Mom," Jared responded immediately afterwards.

Myles began to tear into the hearty breakfast that was before him while Jared took his time enjoying and savoring every morsel.

"Are you guys ready for your first day at your new school?" Mrs. Taylor asked.

"As ready as I'll ever be!" Myles excitedly answered.

"Yeah. Yippee," Jared sarcastically added.

"Jared, just make the best of the situation," Mrs. Taylor lovingly advised. "I know you're sad about leaving your friends at your old school, but you'll make new ones. I promise you. Just wait and see.

"And your big brother will be there to look out for you," Mr. Taylor added.

"Yeah… like always," Myles stalely responded.

"Boys," Mrs. Taylor began.

Both Myles and Jared knew that Mrs. Taylor's tone of voice meant that it was time for reaffirmation when it came to their family's life purpose.

"God has truly blessed us," she continued. "Your father has been given this awesome opportunity to start his own construction firm."

"I've always wanted to own and operate my own business," Mr. Taylor added.

"And as a family, we *must*, and we *will* support one another," Mrs. Taylor reaffirmed.

Mr. Taylor got up from his chair and stood next his sons. He lightly touched them on their shoulders in love. "I know it's going to be a big adjustment coming here from L.A., but everything is going to be fine. We're going to be just fine."

"Yes, I know I will be, Pops," Myles happily responded. "I am ready to begin the start of my new life, and I am already determined to make the best of this situation."

"Thank you, Myles," Mr. Taylor said. Then, he looked over to his younger son. "Jared?"

"Yes, sir. I'll try," Jared replied trying to sound as confident as his older brother.

"That's all we ask," Mrs. Taylor responded. "Honey, do you want anything specific for breakfast?"

"No, just a cup of coffee, please," Mr. Taylor said to his wife.

"I'll get that for you. Boys, you two better get on to school. You don't want to be late on your first day."

Jared and Myles finished eating the last little bit of food that was left on their plates. After they finished, Myles immediately grabbed his bookbag from the floor and looked inside to make sure he had everything he needed to ensure that his first day was a success. Jared picked up his bookbag and hugged his mother sadly. Mrs. Taylor could sense that her baby boy was having a hard time adjusting to the major change in their family's life. She kissed Jared on the cheek.

"Have a good day, sweetie," she said to Jared trying to assure him that everything would be fine.

"Okay," Jared responded. "Bye, Dad."

"See you later, son," Mr. Taylor said as he watched Jared exit the dining room.

Myles zipped up his bookbag happily and began to make his way towards his brand-new life, but he could feel his father's grip on his arm. Myles turned around towards his father. "Yes, Pops?" he wondered.

"Please make sure you look after your little brother. He's going to need you today."

"Don't I always?" Myles replied with a big smile.

"Yes, you do," Mr. Taylor answered.

"Bye, Mom! Bye, Dad! Love you guys!"

"Love you too," they both responded as Myles excitedly exited the dining room.

Mr. and Mrs. Taylor looked at each other with worry and concern as they could hear both of their sons leaving the house.

Myles and Jared made their way down the sidewalk towards their new school. Jared slowly followed behind his older brother in the hopes that he could prolong the inevitable. After a few seconds, Myles turned around and could see that his younger brother was lagging behind. "Would you hurry up? You're going to make us late!" Myles nagged.

Jared just blew his breath in frustration as he tried to force himself to catch up to Myles.

"I can't believe we're walking to school," Jared whined.

"The school's only a few blocks away from the house. Makes sense to walk. It saves money on gas," Myles responded.

"Whatever."

"Listen, Jared, now I know that you are probably nervous about being the new kid at this school. So am I, but we can't let these kids know that. We have to show them that the new kids have come to rule the school. We have to take the popularity we had on the West Coast and bring it down here to the Dirty South."

"See that's the thing. I never was popular at our old school. Yeah, I had my group of friends, but I was never as popular as you were."

"Okay. Then, think of this as a fresh start. Come on, man. I need for you to man up and start looking out for yourself."

"And what about you?" Jared wondered.

"Look, little brother, starting at a new school in the middle of the school year takes a lot of work. Things are already established at this place, which makes it harder for someone as determined as me to make this high school my home," Myles explained.

Jared blew his breath in frustration as he continued to listen to Myles yammer on.

Myles continued, "So, I'm going to need all my energy to focus on me and building my reputation. I can't use all my time protecting you. Do you understand?"

"Yeah, I understand," Jared responded. "You're selfish!"

"I'm not selfish. I'm just helping you have faith in yourself and finally teaching you how to stand up on your own two feet."

"Yeah, whatever."

As they continued to walk, Jared noticed a homeless man sitting up against the wall of the judicial court building. He watched as he waved his cup hoping for a generous soul to give to him. Jared could see the different people walking past the homeless man without even acknowledging his presence.

"Please! Please, help the homeless! I need food!" the homeless man cried out as a businessman talking on his cell phone walked past him. "Please, sir, help me out! I haven't eaten in weeks!"

"Get a job!" the businessman yelled continuing to make his way down the sidewalk.

Jared watched in disbelief as a mother holding the hand of her young daughter walked by the homeless man. The little girl could see the man.

"Look, Mommy," she said. "That man is homeless! Let's give him some money!"

"Come along, sweetie. We're not going to support his drug habit," the mother responded quickly walking away from the homeless man slightly dragging her daughter along with her. Jared could see the little girl looking back at the homeless man and the homeless man looking sadly back at her.

Myles and Jared continued to walk down the sidewalk as they began to pass the homeless man.

"Please, young sirs, can you please spare some change?" he asked.

Jared and Myles stopped and looked at each other. They looked down at the homeless man, and he looked up at them with sadness and desperation in his eyes. Jared pulled out some change from his pocket. He looked to see that all he had was a couple of quarters, several nickels, and five pennies. Jared placed all that he had in the homeless man's cup. The homeless man looked at Jared and smiled, and Jared smiled back at him.

Myles pulled out a dollar from his pocket and placed it in the homeless man's cup as well.

"Thank you, young sirs," the homeless man said.

"You're welcome," Jared responded.

"May God bless you, sir," Myles added.

As Myles and Jared began to walk away, the homeless man watched the young boys. Suddenly, a gold twinkle brightly lit up in both of his eyes as he watched them from afar.

Jared had a good feeling inside of him. He realized that he had done something good, something that could change someone's life for the better. Maybe today would not be as bad as he thought. Jared turned around to look for the homeless man, but he realized that no one was behind him. Jared stopped in amazement. He looked around and saw no one. The homeless man was gone.

Myles continued to walk, but suddenly, he stopped realizing that his little brother was no longer with him. Myles looked and walked back to Jared, who was looking around lost and confused.

"Jared, why did you stop walking?" Myles asked.

"Where did the homeless man go?" Jared wondered.

“I don’t know,” Myles responded. “He’s probably moved on to another area. Now, come on here. We’re almost late for school.”

Myles resumed making his way towards the school. Jared looked again at the area where they had the encounter with the homeless man, but no one was there. Jared shook his head in confusion and sighed, and he hurriedly rushed towards his brother as they made their way towards the beginning of their new life.

CHAPTER TWO

The hallways of Rowlands High School were crawling with students, teachers, and faculty members walking up and down the hallways. Several students were standing next to their lockers talking and laughing. It was the typical high school scene where the cool kids wanted to be seen and heard while the not so cool kids did their best to remain invisible to avoid any ridicule that could come their way.

The doors swung open as Jared and Myles walked in observing their surroundings. They could see that things were going to be a lot different here than what they were used to.

“Well,” Myles began as they continued to look around, “here we are. Rowlands High School.”

“Yippee,” Jared sarcastically responded.

“Look, Jared, I hated moving as much as you did, but there’s nothing we can do about it now. So, let’s live for today and enjoy the ride. Now, are you going to be able to find your classes?"

"Yeah, I'm good. Now, go and make a name for yourself."

"Wish me luck," Myles said with a smile as he walked away from his brother.

Jared sighed as he watched Myles walk into the abyss that was their new high school. Jared pulled out a piece of paper from his pocket. He looked at it and then started looking around.

"241. Locker 241," he said to himself as he walked away in the opposite direction trying to locate his new home for the remainder of the school year.

Jared continued to mumble to himself as if the search for his locker was never-ending. After minutes of trying to locate that magic number, he looked up and finally saw them. "241," he said to himself as he opened his locker and began placing the contents of his bookbag inside of it.

As he was unpacking, Jared looked over and saw a fifteen-year-old young lady standing beside him and looking at him with a big, bright smile. "Hi," she greeted.

"Hello," Jared replied. He did not really know how to react to this. A pretty girl had never been the first one to speak to him before.

"My name is Naomi," she said holding her hand out.

"Jared," he nervously responded shaking her hand. *God, please don't let my hand start sweating.*

Jared looked up into Naomi's big, brown eyes. He began to smile as he began to get lost in her beauty. Naomi smiled as she slowly began to release her hand from his. Jared did not want this moment to end, but he knew that if he did not want to appear as being weird, he should let go.

"I've never seen you around before. Are you new here?" Naomi asked.

"Yep. I'm the new kid in town."

"That's cool. It's always cool being in a new town and in a new school. You have an opportunity to start over."

"Yeah. Right," Jared responded not really being open to the possibilities of having to start over.

"Trust me," Naomi continued. "Having everyone know who you are and what you've done is not the best thing in the world."

"Understandable, but the best thing for me right now is if I wasn't here at all."

"I feel you," Naomi agreed.

Jared sighed as he resumed placing his belongings inside his locker. Suddenly, Naomi had a sly and mischievous smile on her face. She looked at Jared and said, "You don't want to be here… And I don't want to be here... So, how about we just skip school?"

Jared could not believe what he was hearing. "Did you just say skip school?"

"Yeah!" Naomi exclaimed.

"I don't know," Jared responded in uncertainty in his voice.

"Come on, Jared," Naomi pressured. "My philosophy is do what you feel. And since we don't *feel* like being here, we should leave.

Jared began to think about what Naomi was saying. She had such a sweet voice and such a beautiful smile. How could he reject the suggestions of what appeared to be his only friend at his new school?

"Okay," he answered. "I like that philosophy. Let's do it."

Jared and Naomi both grabbed their bookbags and closed their lockers.

"Remember," Naomi warned. "Act normal."

Jared nodded his head as they both acted like they were walking towards a classroom. Then, they continued to the nearest exit. Quickly and quietly, Naomi opened the door, and they both walked out of the school not worrying about a care in the world – well, at least for that moment.

Myles continued down the other side of the hallway searching for his locker. He looked up to see the numbers 1235. He smiled as he looked down the hall. He saw the most incredible sight – a stunning young lady with long, dark hair with several flecks of golden highlights, beautiful green eyes, and pearly white teeth that would make someone go blind if they stared too long.

Myles slowly began to approach this magnificent beauty, who was standing at her locker looking through a notepad. When he made his way to her, he cleared his throat catching the young lady's attention. "Hi," he said.

"Hello," she responded.

"My name is Myles Taylor. And you are---"

"Brittany Kirkpatrick," she introduced.

Myles gently grabbed Brittany's hand and softly kissed it. Brittany giggled a little bit, but she caught herself after she realized what just happened and tried to disguise it with a cough.

"Why did you do that?" Brittany asked.

"A true gentleman always kisses the hand of a lady… especially a beautiful one such as yourself."

"Well, thank you," Brittany said trying to pretend to not be flattered. "And where exactly are you from, Mr. Myles Taylor?'

"I'm from Los Angeles."

"And why are you here?"

"Because my father got the opportunity to move down here to start his own construction firm."

"That's pretty awesome!" Brittany replied.

"I didn't think so at first," Myles truthfully responded. "It's hard leaving your friends and your familiar surroundings."

"Yeah."

"But now, after meeting you," Myles continued as he inched his way closer towards Brittany, "I think I'm *definitely* going to like it here."

Brittany smiled.

Suddenly, a thunderous voice came from behind her. "And who is your new friend, babe?"

Brittany turned around as a 5'11", athletically built young man walked up to her wearing a letterman's jacket and carrying a basketball under his arm. Myles watched as what looked to him to be a basketball player put his arm around Brittany.

"Oh! Daniel! Hey!" Brittany said in a flustered tone. "This is… this is.... um…"

"Myles Taylor," he interjected holding his hand out.

"He's from Los Angles," Brittany added.

"I'm Daniel Richards," the young man responded as he grabbed Myles hand tightly and tried to squeeze it with all his might. "I'm Brittany's boyfriend."

Myles felt the tightness in Daniel's grip, but he was not about to let this kid think he could not hang with the best of them. So, Myles matched the firmness of Daniel's grip as they both locked eyes looking for any sign of weakness. Brittany watched with nervousness as the boys continued to hold on tightly. When both Myles and Daniel realized that neither one of them was backing down, they both began to let each other go slowly, each still trying to "best" the other even to the last second.

"Well, I better get on to homeroom," Brittany said after both Myles and Daniel finally released each other's hands. She turned to Daniel and kissed him on the cheek and continued, "I'll see you at first period."

"Okay, babe," Daniel responded still glaring at Myles. "See you later."

Brittany closed her locker and turned to Myles. "It was nice meeting you."

"Nice meeting you, too," he said with a smile.

Both Myles and Daniel watched as Brittany walked away from them and down the hallway. Myles sighed and began to walk back to his locker, but he could feel Daniel's hand grabbing him tightly on the shoulder and forcefully turning him around.

"Listen, here," Daniel began.

"You better get your hands off me!" Myles yelled pushing Daniel away from him.

"Look, here, punk, I'm only going to tell you once," Daniel threatened. "Stay away from my girl."

"And who do you think you are?" Myles challenged.

"I told you. I'm Daniel Richards."

"Well, Daniel Richards, I don't care who you are. This is a free country, and I can talk to anyone I want to."

"Well, I think you'll change your tune when I talk to the mayor," Daniel responded with a smirk.

Daniel's response had Myles a little confused. "The mayor?" he wondered. "You're going to talk to the mayor… about a girl?"

"No," Myles responded. "I'm going to talk to him about your father's construction firm."

"How did you---"

"The mayor of Garden City is my father," Daniel revealed. "I know everything about you, your family, and your father's business. So, unless you want your father's business to start off as a failure, I suggest you do what I say and stay away from my girl… DUDE."

Daniel walked away from Myles forcefully brushing past him with his shoulder. Myles angrily watched as Daniel walked away. Myles sighed in frustration and returned to his locker realizing that his first day in this school may not be as easy and trouble-free as he thought.

CHAPTER THREE

Deirdre Clayton, better known to very few as Deek, was a sixteen-year-old girl who walked to the beat of her own sarcastic, gloomy, negative drum. She wore all black clothing and black boots with small spikes. Her hair was jet black, and she wore black lipstick, black eyeliner, and black nail polish. Deek walked down the hallways of Rowlands High School as she always did – alone and invisible.

As she made her way down the roaming halls of discontent and resistant, Deek could hear the whispers and laughs and feel the stares of the other students that were looking at her with disgust and repulsion.

"Look at her. She's so weird."

"It's people like her that make me sick."

"She's such a freak. I wish she would just go away."

It was same thing every second of every minute of every hour of every day. She had heard it all before, but that didn't make the fact that no one in that school liked her go away. That did not make the hurt and pain from all the rejection disappear. As the whispers and laughs continued, Deek did everything she could to hold back her tears. She refused to let what she heard get to her. So, she did what she always did. She rolled her eyes and continued to walk down the hallway pretending to ignore the entire negative world that surrounded her.

As Deek passed the front office, she could see a man wearing glasses that were held together by duct tape, a colorful striped shirt with an even more colorful polka-dot bow tie, khaki pants that came just slightly above his ankles, and worn-out loafers that looked as if they could tear at any minute. Deek watched as the man was struggling to carry a huge stack of folders and papers. He appeared to be stumbling at every step. Deek looked as some of her classmates walked past him talking and laughing at every twitch he made trying not to drop all his paperwork. The man walked in front of a classroom, and suddenly, the door opened widely knocking the teacher and all his folders and papers to the floor. Deek watched in horror as the man struggled to get up and gather his things.

A teacher walked out the classroom and sees the man on the floor trying to pick everything up. “You shouldn’t have been in front of the door!” she snapped as she slammed the door and walked away.

Deek began to have pity for the man as he desperately tried to pick up the folders and papers that were sprawled all over the floor. Deek saw how some of the students and even some of the teachers and faculty members walked past him laughing and pointing.

“Please… please… can somebody help me?” he begged. “I’m going to be late for my homeroom class.”

But no one heard his cries. No one heard his pleas. They just ignored him. They just continued as if he was just another non-existent person who was not worth caring about. Deek knew how that felt. She experienced it every second of every minute of every hour of every day.

Deek sighed and walked over to the man as he continued to gather his things. She kneeled in front of him. The man looked up at Deek, and Deek looked at him. Deek smiled a little barely showing any teeth, and she could see the man smiling back at her. Deek began picking up the papers and putting them inside the folders. The man watched as this good Samaritan stopped what she was doing to help him.

After a few minutes, they both finished picking up everything. Deek handed the man the stack of folders and papers that she collected. He took them and said, “Thank you.”

Deek looked him in his eyes, but she did not say anything. She sighed and resumed walking down the hallway.

“Remember, God loves you!” he shouted.

“Yeah, right,” she mumbled. “No one else does.”

The man watched Deek walk away in sadness. Suddenly, a gold twinkle brightly lit up in both of his eyes. He turned around and carefully walked towards the main office.

The main office appeared to be a disaster area as teenagers were moving in and out. Some faculty members were fighting over who was going to use the copy machine while others were struggling to work the fax machine. The principal’s office door opened, and Principal James Lawson stormed out looking around at the melee that was right before his eyes. He tried to make his way through the pandemonium as he walked up to the administrative assistant, who was sitting at her desk trying to figure out what exactly was going on.

"Principal Lawson, can you explain to me what in the world is happening right now?" she asked.

"Well, Kim, since Hawthorne High School burned down last semester, the Board of Education mandated that we house them temporarily," Principal Lawson explained. "More students meant more faculty members, which means just a big ole mess."

"A big ole mess that we have to house in this little space," Kim added.

"Clearly," Principal Lawson sarcastically expressed. "Anyway, I have a meeting with the new superintendent of the district. And I'm already late for it."

"I'll try and hold down the fort," Kim encouraged.

Principal Lawson sighed and began to make his way through the crowd of people entering and exiting the office. He closed the door and walked out.

As he made his way towards the school door exit, he bumped into the man who was carrying the papers and folders. "I'm sorry," Principal Lawson apologized.

"That's okay, can you---"

But before he could finish, Principal Lawson rushed out the door. The man sighed as he looked around watching different teachers and students walking past him.

"Excuse me," he asked hoping that someone would stop and listen. "Can you please help? This is my first day, and I'm a little lost. I need to find room 175. I'm going to be late for my homeroom class. Can someone please help me?"

But no one did. No one stopped to help. No one paid attention to the desperation in his voice. The man sighed in discouragement, but then, he looked up and saw Brittany walking towards him. "Excuse me, young lady, can you please help me?"

"Sure," she said with her big, bright smile. "What do you need?"

"I'm a little lost, and this is my first day. Can you point me in the direction of room 175?"

"Oh, that's my boyfriend's homeroom class!" Brittany responded. "Yes, just turn around and continue down that hallway and make your first right. It'll be the first door on your left."

"Thank you, young lady," the man happily said with gratitude.

"No problem," she replied. "I hope you have a good first day."

Brittany smiled again and walked away. The man delighted in her smile. As he watched her disappear into the sea of other students, that same gold twinkle brightly lit up in both of his eyes. Then, he turned around and walked down the hallway as the bell rang.

After minutes of searching and carefully carrying his belongings, he was able to find the correct classroom: room 175. He took a deep breath and opened the door. As he entered the classroom, he could not believe what was right before his eyes. All the students were talking and laughing obnoxiously loud. The man instantly saw the separation among this group of young angst. The cheerleaders and the ones that some may call the most popular were in the middle of the classroom while the jocks, including Daniel, were sitting in the back of the class. The "less popular" students were sitting in their seats quietly trying to ignore the constant taunting that they continued to hear on a daily basis.

The man sighed and walked over to the desk. He dropped all his papers and folders on his desk, which seemed to spread all over the place. The man fixed his glasses and looked at his surroundings, but no one seemed to notice that he was even in the room.

"Good morning," he began. "My name is Michael Angelo, but you can just call me, Michael."

The students did not even acknowledge his presence. They continued to talk and laugh ignoring everything Michael was saying.

"Excuse me, students," Michael continued. "May I have your attention, please?"

But no one paid attention. It was as if Michael was talking to a brick wall. A defeated look appeared on Michael's face. He sadly sat down at his desk and sighed. Daniel was laughing with his classmates, but then, he looked up and saw Michael sitting at the desk looking down.

Daniel stood up and sighed, and he courageously walked to the front of the classroom. "Hey, hey, hey!" he yelled.

No one seemed to pay attention to Daniel either.

"QUIET!" he screamed.

Suddenly, everyone stopped talking and laughing. It was so quiet that one could hear a pin drop. Michael watched as all the students looked at Daniel as if he was the leader of the herd. "Look," Daniel began. "Now, we're being very disrespectful right now. This nice man is trying to tell us something, and it may be important. Now, let's keep it real. We wouldn't dare treat Mrs. Milledge like this. So, let's show---"

Daniel turned to Michael and asked, "What's your name again?"

"Michael."

"Michael," Daniel continued to his classmates. "Let's show Michael the same respect. Okay? Can we do that?"

All the students mumbled either "yeah", "sure", or "okay."

"Good," Daniel responded. Then, he turned to Michael and said, "It's all yours, Mike."

Michael proudly stood up and replied, "Thank you, Daniel."

Daniel had a confused look on his face. "How did you know my name?" he asked.

Michael smiled and held up one of his folders. "Your file," he answered. "Matters of fact, I have all your files, and I know each and every one of you. And I want each of you to know me. My name is Michael, and I will be substituting for Mrs. Milledge. Now, before the bell rings for homeroom to end, I just want to urge you to---"

Suddenly, the bell rang. Everyone, except Michael and Daniel, got up from their desks and walked out of the classroom talking about what had just transpired the last few minutes.

"Never mind," Michael said under his breath.

He sighed as Daniel walked to his desk and picked up his basketball and bookbag. He walked up to Michael and touched Michael's shoulder. "Don't worry, man. Your day will get better."

Daniel smiled at Michael, and Michael smiled back. Then, Daniel walked out of the classroom. As Daniel was leaving, Michael took off his glasses, and suddenly, the same gold twinkle that he had before lit up brightly in both of his eyes.

As Daniel walked down the hallway away from his homeroom class, he stopped in his tracks. He did not know why he stopped, but something inside of him was telling him to go back inside the classroom. He did not know what it was, but he knew that the urge was too strong to ignore. Daniel sighed, turned around, and walked back to his homeroom class.

"And another thing," Daniel began as he re-entered the classroom, but to his amazement, no one was there. Michael was gone. The folders and the papers were gone. It was as if no one had even stepped foot inside the room. Daniel looked around in amazement and confusion wondering what exactly was happening here. "Where'd he go?"

Daniel could not fathom in the recesses of his mind where Michael went or how he could have just "disappeared" from the classroom. After a few more seconds of pondering, Daniel shrugged his shoulders and walked out of the classroom closing the door behind him resuming to his everyday life.

CHAPTER FOUR

"Oooooh, this ice cream definitely tastes so much better in the morning!" Naomi exclaimed as she was walking down the street finishing her strawberry ice cream.

"I wonder why," Jared responded following behind her and enjoying his cookies and cream scoop.

"Probably because you're not supposed to have it in the morning," she laughed.

"I guess things always taste better when they are *forbidden*."

"Exactly," Naomi responded in a very flirtatious manner, and then, she flashed a smile.

Jared shyly smiled back. He knew that skipping class was not the right thing to do, but he was happy that he had made a friend: a pretty friend at that. He could not believe that this beautiful young lady wanted to spend time with him, but he knew that he would take advantage of every minute of it.

Jared and Naomi continued to walk down the sidewalk talking and laughing. As Jared continued to marvel in Naomi's presence, he suddenly became distracted by what appeared to be a horrifying sight. An elderly man was standing bent over on the sidewalk. The elderly man was reaching out for help, but several people ignored his pleas for assistance.

"Can someone please help me? I need help crossing the street." Jared could hear the elderly man ask.

A runner in a bright blue jump suit jogged past the old man not even flinching at the fact that he was begging for help.

Talking on her cell phone, a woman dressed in an exquisite designer business pants suit walked up to the elderly man. She stood beside him disregarding this man's desperate cries. The elderly man subtly and gently tugged at her jacket asking, "Excuse me, miss… can you please help me across the street?"

The woman looked at him with a disgusted look on her face and quickly snatched away from him. "Let go of me!" she shouted as she quickly walked across the street continuing to talk on her cell phone.

Jared and Naomi watched in disheartenment. They looked at each other and gave each other a signal because they knew what they needed to do. Jared took Naomi's leftover ice cream and threw his and hers in the trash can next to them. Then, they slowly walked up to the elderly man. He looked up at them with his big, sad, brown eyes. "Excuse me… can you young people please help an elderly man across the street?" he dejectedly asked.

"Of course," Naomi happily responded. "Come on, Jared."

"Okay," Jared replied as he lightly grabbed the elderly man's right arm.

The elderly man smiled as Naomi grabbed his left arm. Then, Naomi and Jared slowly walked across the street with him making sure that the elderly man did not miss a beat as he slowly and steadily crossed from one side to the other. After a few minutes, they finally got to the other side. When they finished, Naomi and Jared released the man's arms, and the man looked at both teens and smiled brightly. "Thank you," he said.

"No problem," Jared responded with a smile.

"Um… shouldn't you kids be in school?" the elderly man wondered.

Naomi and Jared nervously looked at each other. Jared did not know what to say, but Naomi knew the perfect way out of this situation would be to lie her way out. So, she answered, "We're not in school today, sir, because there is no school today. Today's a school holiday! Right, Jared?" she asked looking for reassurance.

"Um… right, right," Jared said. He never was a good liar. But he had to say something to back Naomi up.

"Do you need any help getting anywhere else?" Naomi asked.

"No," the elderly man said. "Thank you, again."

Jared then began to really look the elderly man. He studied the features on his face. He knew that he had seen those eyes before, but he just could not remember where. While Jared was studying the elderly man, he could feel Naomi tugging on his shirt. "Come on, Jared. Let's go," she urged.

Naomi pulled Jared along, but Jared could not take his eyes off the elderly man. But after several saves from running into different objects on the sidewalk, Jared decided to look away from the elderly man, and he continued walking and talking with Naomi. But he could not shake the feeling. There was something familiar about that elderly man, but he just could not put his finger on it. Naomi saw the troubled look on Jared's face.

"What's wrong with you, Jared?" she wondered.

"Nothing, it's just... I feel like I've seen that elderly man somewhere before. And his voice… His voice sounded very familiar. I think I know him."

"You're just being paranoid about this whole skipping school thing," Naomi tried to rationalize. "Stick with me, kid. I got some much more to show you. Let's go!"

Naomi grabbed Jared's hand. *I can't believe she's holding my hand*, he excitedly thought as she pulled him along with him.

The elderly man continued to watch Jared and Naomi as they happily walked down the sidewalk foot loose and carefree. It was as if they did not have a care or trouble in the world. But as the elderly man was watching them, he began to stand up straight. Suddenly, that same gold twinkle lit up brightly in both of his eyes.

As Jared and Naomi continued to walk down the street, that feeling would not go away. It was as if it was tugging at Jared's heart. *What if...*

Jared suddenly turned around to look at the elderly man once more, but when he turned around, the elderly man was gone. Nowhere in sight! It was as if he had disappeared into thin air just like the homeless man he and Myles had encountered earlier.

Naomi looked and could see that Jared was once again lagging behind. She grabbed his arm and said, "Come on here, boy!"

A green 2001 Honda slowly pulled up into the parking lot. After the loud engine finally shut off, the driver's side door opened, and Principal Lawson stepped out of the car. When he closed the door, he looked at the magnificent skyscraper that was before him. He looked in amazement because it was nothing he had ever seen before. It was as if it was overlooking the entire city. After he snapped back into reality, he took a deep breath and walked toward the building not knowing what awaited him on the inside.

A strapping, alluring, young man was standing at the window overlooking his surroundings. He watched the city streets through his dark shades as if he was preparing to oversee an upcoming conquest. Suddenly, his gaze was interrupted by several knocks at the door. The young man cleared his throat and called out, "Come in!"

The door of the boardroom opened, and Principal Lawson slowly walked in. "Mr. Malo?"

"Principal Lawson," Mr. Malo responded still looking out of the window. "Please close the door and come have a seat."

Principal Lawson closed the door and slowly walked to the first chair nearest to him. However, Principal Lawson seemed a little uneasy as he noticed that Mr. Malo did not look at him to acknowledge his presence. He watched as Mr. Malo continued to stare out into the scenery.

After a few more seconds of awkward silence, Principal Lawson cleared his throat and began, "Well, Mr. Malo... I am here today---"

"Yes," Mr. Malo interrupted in an authoritative manner as he finally turned around towards Principal Lawson. "Let's discuss the reason you are here today... Principal Lawson."

Principal Lawson began to grow a little nervous as he realized Mr. Malo's commanding stature in his black suit and shirt and red tie. Principal Lawson cleared his throat again. “Yes. I... um,” he continued trying to gain his composure, “I am starting to realize that it is getting to a point to where I am unable to recognize students from faculty or to determine who belongs at our school and who doesn’t. It is just pandemonium. We need structure... we need order. I went to the superintendent for help, and he referred me to you… I mean, he should be the one actually providing the assistance, but he’s nothing but a sorry, good for nothing… Anyway, this is why I came to you and your company, Mr. Malo. I was told that your company produces and provides the best, quality identification badges.”

“And you were told correctly, Mr. Lawson,” Mr. Malo responded confidently. “Our company can provide the quality you need that’ll help bring back the structure that you desire in your school.

“How soon can we have these ID badges?” Principal Lawson wondered.

“As soon as you need them,” Mr. Malo quickly replied. “We at Emblem Validation Insignia Licensing believe in quality, FAST service.”

“We have over one-thousand students and one hundred faculty members. When can you have the badges completed?”

"I guarantee them by noon today."

Principal Lawson had a puzzled look on his face. "Are you serious?"

Mr. Malo slowly walked up to Principal Lawson. Principal Lawson nervously gulped as Mr. Malo's commanding, yet intimidating presence moved closer towards him. Mr. Malo looked down at Principal Lawson, and Principal Lawson could clearly see his anxious reflection in Mr. Malo's sharp, clean shades.

"I told you," Mr. Malo repeated sternly. "We at Emblem Validation Insignia Licensing believe in quality, FAST service."

"You know what," Principal Lawson said as he stood up to re-gain his poise, but he began to think about what Mr. Malo said with a concerned look on his face. "I was so anxious to get a solution to our school's problem that I never realized that if you put together the first letters of each word in your company's name - Emblem Validation Insignia Licensing - that it spells... EVIL.

Mr. Malo smiled and responded, "Just a coincidence."

This caught Principal Lawson off guard. He was convinced that this man had no idea how to smile or if he ever smiled a day in his life.

"So... Principal Lawson," Mr. Malo continued as he reached his hand out towards Principal Lawson. "Do we have a deal?"

Principal Lawson hesitated for a second as he looked at Mr. Malo with suspicion in his eyes. He was not completely sure if this was the move that he should be making. Something felt... off. However, instead of listening to that small voice inside of him, Principal Lawson smiled and reached his hand out shaking Mr. Malo's hand. "We have a deal," Principal Lawson happily said. "I will call my office manager as soon as I walk out of here and have her e-mail all the names of all the students and faculty at our school."

"Thank you," Mr. Malo said, "and we will hand-deliver the badges to your school by noon so that way all of your students and your faculty will have them before they go home today."

"Okay. Well, I look forward to it. Thank you, Mr. Malo. Thank you."

"No, Principal Lawson," Mr. Malo said with a sly grin, "thank you."

Principal Lawson smiled back, but there was a small sliver of doubt in the back of his mind about the decision he just made. However, he realized he had to live with his choice as he began to walk away from Mr. Malo and walked out of the conference room closing the door behind him.

After Principal Lawson exited, Mr. Malo's grin became more sinister and more malevolent as he took off his shades, and his eye sockets were glowing bright red revealing himself to be Nefarious in human form. "The time... HAS COME!" Nefarious gruesomely snarled as he menacingly cackled.

CHAPTER FIVE

Anticipation and eagerness began to exude as Myles sat on the bench anxiously watching the other guys on the court playing a scrimmage game of basketball. Myles began to zero in on Daniel, who was on the defensive side wearing a blue vest. Daniel smiled confidently while guarding the opposing team member, who was wearing a red vest. Myles continued to study Daniel; every move Daniel made, Myles internalized it so that when his moment came, he would be ready to go up against Daniel.

FWEEEEEET!

The sound of the coach blowing the whistle was heard across the gym signifying the game was now in play.

One of the boys on the red team began to dribble the ball down the court while the other four dispersed under the basketball hoop with the blue team, including Daniel, guarding their every move. The young man running the ball started to look for someone who was open, but it appeared that no one was available in sight for him to pass the ball to. However, one of his teammates broke free from the young man on the blue team who was guarding him. The dribbler saw his teammate, and he immediately threw the ball towards him with all his might. Suddenly, Daniel broke away from the guy he was guarding and jumped in front of the young man who was about to catch the ball. Daniel intercepted the pass. Then, Daniel quickly dashed towards the other side of the court. The red team tried to catch up to him, but it was to no avail. Daniel continued to run as if the wind was pushing him giving him the extra momentum that he needed, and then, he leaped and placed the ball inside the hoop producing a nice, clean lay-up.

After the ball successfully went through the hoop, Daniel landed gracefully on the floor with a huge grin on his face. Myles noticed the smug expression on Daniel's face. *Look at him*, Myles thought. *He thinks he's all that. Just give me a chance. I'll show him.*

"Good job, Richards!" Coach Beane yelled out.

"Don't I know it!" Daniel arrogantly responded. "Nobody can touch my game!"

"We'll see about that," Coach Beane chortled as he looked over at the young men sitting on the sidelines noticing Myles, who was observing intensively. "New guy!"

Myles looked over at Coach Beane with a confused look on his face. "Um... you talking to me?"

"You're the only new guy here," Coach Beane responded sarcastically. "Suit up! You're going in on the red team, and you'll be guarding Richards."

Myles smiled confidently as he ran out into the court.

"Stephenson, come in!" the coach shouted.

One of the guys took off his red vest, gave it to Myles, and walked off the court. Myles put on his red vest on while Daniel walked up to him. "This is going to be good," Daniel sneered. "I already schooled you about my girl... and now, I get to school you on the court."

"Let's see how your walk matches your talk," Myles replied as he picked up the basketball from the ground and forcefully threw it at Daniel, causing him to catch it with a little difficulty.

Daniel slyly smiled as he began to dribble the ball. "Get ready to get your ankles broke," he jeered.

Boom. Boom. Boom.

Myles watched Daniel intensely as he could hear the ball being bounced on the hardwood floor. Daniel glared at Myles trying to intimidate him; however, Myles continued to keep his focus on the task at hand. Daniel tried to do a fancy move: a quick triple step that he saw some professional basketball player do trying to show off. However, Myles was able to keep up with him; he was not fazed at all by the "tricks" Daniel was trying to do.

Suddenly, Daniel tried a swift step in order to break away from Myles, but Myles was two steps ahead of him. Daniel ran down the court breaking through the opposite team, who was now guarding the basketball hoop, but Myles darted behind him. Daniel jumped up to do another lay-up, but Myles met him where he was jumping up with him, blocking the ball out of Daniel's hands, and knocking the ball to the ground.

As they both landed back on the ground, Myles quickly grabbed the ball and began to run dribbling it down the opposite end of the court. Daniel, now stunned at what just occurred, quickly snapped back into reality and began to chase Myles down the court with all his strength. However, Daniel's will to not allow Myles to humiliate him proved to be successful as Daniel began to guard Myles after catching up to him. Myles continued to bounce the ball watching and studying Daniel, as Daniel attempted to keep up with Myles. Myles, then, smiled noticing a flaw in Daniel's stance. Suddenly, Myles did a move forcing Daniel to move in one direction, but Myles moved in the opposite direction faking Daniel out. After breaking away from Daniel, Myles jumped up and slam-dunked the basketball into the hoop.

As Myles landed back on the ground, the entire gym erupted into shouts and cheers as both the red and blue team, along with the players who were sitting on the bench, ran up to Myles celebrating what just took place. Daniel watched with anger as he watched everyone praise Myles.

Myles smiled with happiness and exuberance as Coach Beane walked up to him. "Excellent job, new kid!" he exclaimed. "That was excellent foot work!"

"Thank you, sir," Myles blissfully replied.

Then, Coach Beane turned to Daniel. "Looks like the new kid in town is going to take your spot, Richards. You better step your game up."

Daniel irately sighed.

"Alright, boys. Hit the showers!" Coach Beane yelled as he and the other boys walked off the court leaving Myles and Daniel standing there alone.

Myles licked his lips and smiled as he walked up to Daniel. Myles saw the anger on Daniel's face, but he did not care. Myles enjoyed being able to stick it to him. "Now... THAT'S how you let your walk match your talk," Myles taunted as if he was taking the knife and twisting it even further into Daniel's bruised ego.

Daniel continued to glare at Myles with a pissed look on his face as Myles began to laugh to himself and started walking away. After Myles exited, Daniel breathed angrily as he watched the basketball rolling towards him. Daniel picked up the ball and held in his hand for a few seconds feeling its touch as if he was internalizing his defeat. Suddenly, Daniel forcefully threw the ball against the wall and continued to pant with anger.

A huge cloud of black smoke filled the sky as Deek sat on a bench holding her lit cigarette right outside the door of the school. Deek looked around and surveyed her surroundings. Then, she sighed heavily as she resumed smoking the cigarette as if she was trying to relieve herself of the stress that constantly filled what she believed was her empty life. As she inhaled, Deek looked and saw Naomi and Jared walking down the sidewalk talking. Deek rolled her eyes as she blew out the smoke from her mouth.

"We are back at a perfect time," Naomi said to Jared. "It's almost time for lunch, and we can just sneak right on in."

"Yeah. I guess," Jared said with a subdued look on his face.

"Now wasn't that a whole lot better than going to class?"

"I mean, it was... but I must admit that I don't necessarily feel right doing it."

"That's just your conscious. Ignore it. I do it all the time," Naomi nonchalantly stated.

Unbeknownst to Naomi and Jared, Principal Lawson was pulling up in his parking space. As he got out of the car, he saw Naomi and Jared talking with a suspicious look on his face. *Why aren't those two in class?* Principal Lawson wondered as he closed the door and quietly made his way towards them.

"Do you do things like this often?" Jared asked Naomi.

"Sometimes," Naomi admitted.

"Why?" Jared sincerely wondered.

Naomi sighed and replied, "Let's just say that my father is of a... higher authority, and everyone knows it. Everyone around here expects me to be this perfect little princess. It's just hard to live up to the expectations sometimes."

"I'm sure your father doesn't expect you to be perfect."

"Yeah, right," Naomi scoffed as she rolled her eyes.

"Why don't you talk to him about how you're feeling?" Jared suggested.

"And how would I do that?" Naomi questioned with a little attitudinal tone in her voice.

"Well... you can just be honest and tell the truth," Jared responded.

"Why tell the truth when lying about it is so much easier?"

"Because you'll always get caught," Principal Lawson said.

Suddenly, Naomi and Jared turned around in shock at the fact that Principal Lawson was just standing behind them without any warning.

"Hey... Dad," Naomi nervously greeted.

"The principal is your father?" Jared exclaimed.

"That's right," Principal Lawson continued in a stern manner. "And you two just earned yourself a prize trip to the in-house suspension center."

"In-house suspension?" Naomi wondered with a puzzled look on her face. "We don't have that here."

"We do now," Principal Lawson stated. "Let's go! Right now!"

Then, Principal Lawson grabbed Naomi by the arm and shoved Jared in front of him. They walked to the door and walked past Deek, who was still sitting quietly smoking her cigarette watching the entire encounter. Suddenly, Principal Lawson looked at Deek and snatched the cigarette from Deek's mouth, and he threw it on the ground smashing it with his foot.

"You already know," Principal Lawson said to Deek. "Let's go."

"Let me guess," Deek mockingly responded. "Another trip to detention after school."

Ehhhhhhhhhhhhh!

Deek, Naomi, and Jared looked at Principal Lawson with confused glances because of his attempt to make a wrong buzzer noise.

"In-house suspension with these two, Deirdre," Principal Lawson corrected. "Let's go."

Deek sucked her teeth as Principal Lawson opened the door. "Move it!" Principal Lawson forcefully commanded as Jared, Naomi, and Deek slowly and regretfully walked into the school building and the bell rang loudly.

The cafeteria was full of students sitting at the tables eating, talking, and laughing. Daniel was sitting in front of a group of members from the basketball team; however, he was being unusually quiet as he just ate his lunch with a somber look on his face. As Daniel continued to be in his own space, Brittany walked up to the table carrying her lunch tray and sat down in the empty seat next to him. "Hey, baby!" she happily greeted.

"Hey," Daniel responded in a monotone way.

"How was the first half of your day?" Brittany wondered.

"I don't wanna talk about it."

"Oh... what happened?"

"He got schooled!" one of the basketball team members interjected with a laugh.

"By the new kid!" another basketball team member jeered.

"I SAID I DON'T WANT TO TALK ABOUT IT!" Daniel shouted angrily.

"Just because you don't want to talk about it doesn't mean we don't want to talk about it," the first team member responded.

"No. When I say I don't wanna talk about it... that means YOU TOO!" Daniel demanded.

The other basketball team members ignored Daniel's mandate as they continued to snicker and joke among themselves. Meanwhile, Myles began to walk past the table carrying his lunch tray, and Brittany spotted him.

"Hey, Myles," Brittany greeted.

Myles smiled and replied, "How you doin', sweetheart?"

Daniel was now going from anger to rage. *This guy just doesn't know when to quit, does he? I'll show him,* Daniel thought as he held his leg out in front of Myles in a way that Myles would not able to realize what was about to happen.

Still relishing from Brittany's kind gesture towards him, Myles continued to smile while gazing at Brittany's beauty, and not really paying attention to what was right in front of him, Myles proceeded to walk. Suddenly, Myles' leg was caught by Daniel's, causing Myles to trip and fall face down on the floor with all his food from his lunch tray landing in different spots around him. Immediately, everyone, except Brittany, burst out laughing. Myles swiftly hopped up off the ground and rushed up to Daniel; however, Daniel stood up and got in Myles' face.

"Now you don' gone too far," Myles snarled.

"I told you don't talk to my girl again," Daniel scowled.

Myles and Daniel moved as if they were both about to hit each other, but Brittany quickly stood up and inserted herself in between them as the crowd began to boost them up to fight.

"Y'all break it up and stop all of this!" Brittany requested.

However, neither Myles nor Daniel heard her pleas. Both entangled by their anger and dislike for the other,

Myles and Daniel continued glaring angrily at each other. Brittany could see the rage in both of their eyes. Brittany knew that it might be easier to appeal to Myles. "Myles, please," she said to him. "Be the bigger man."

Myles looked into Brittany's beautiful green eyes with the golden flecks, and he could see the sincerity in them. Then, Myles sighed heavily as he kneeled to pick up his tray, and then, he looked back at Daniel and walked away.

"Awwwwwww!" the crowd exclaimed with disappointment.

"That's what I thought, punk!" Daniel shouted as everyone returned to their seats. Myles, ignoring Daniel's ignorant rant, took a seat at a table on the other side of the cafeteria.

Daniel scoffed but was quickly surprised and shocked when he felt a hit on his arm. Daniel looked at Brittany with a confused look on his face. "Why did you hit me?" he wondered.

"Why did you do that to him?" Brittany demanded with disappointment in her voice.

"I told that punk not to mess with you again."

"He wasn't messing with me," Brittany corrected. "I spoke to him, and he was being courteous and speaking back."

"He's feelin' you, Brittany," Daniel informed her.

"So, what?" Brittany responded. "I'm with you, and that's all that matters. Why do you care if he likes me or not?"

"It's a man thing, baby."

"Well, I guess when you become one, you can explain it to me," Brittany mocked.

Daniel was taken aback by Brittany's response. "Oh... it's like that?"

"I'm just saying. Why are you acting all insecure? It's not that serious."

"Oh yeah," Daniel challenged with a sly smile on his face. "That's how you feel?"

"That's how I feel," Brittany stated. "Increase the peace is what I always say."

"Okay," Daniel said as he walked away from Brittany.

Brittany shook her head and sighed as she began to clean up the mess that is on the floor. After she cleaned the floor, she walked towards the garbage bins. Myles watched as Brittany threw everything in the bins. *Maybe I should've helped her with that,* he thought. *But then again, if I'm anywhere near that dude, his face would be smashed in the floor with that spilled food.*

After Brittany finished throwing everything away, she looked over and was very surprised at what she saw. Daniel was talking and laughing with another girl. Brittany could not believe what was happening right in front of her eyes. The girl swung her blond hair around Daniel and was obviously and obnoxiously flirting with him. Suddenly, the girl leaned in and planted a kiss on Daniel's cheek. Brittany's countenance changed from shocked to fury as she stormed over to Daniel.

Daniel and the girl continued to talk and laugh as he looked over and saw Brittany coming towards them. Then, Brittany pushed the girl out the way.

Meanwhile, on the other side of the cafeteria, Myles noticed a big slice of cake on another person's tray that was right in front of him. Myles slowly picked up the cake while that person was not looking. Myles, then, stood up from his seat with the cake and began to approach what was beginning to look like a huge melee.

The blond-headed girl rushed up to Brittany after being forcefully pushed.

"Did you just put your crusty lips on my boyfriend's face?" Brittany angrily asked.

"It's a free country," the other girl rebutted. "I can *kiss* whomever I want."

Then, the girl proceeded to flirtatiously wave at Daniel. Daniel smiled and waved back, which pissed Brittany off even more.

"Well, if you want to kiss something," Brittany said while reaching over and picking up a slice of cake from someone's tray, "kiss this!"

Suddenly, Brittany slammed the piece of cake into the girl's face.

"AHHHHHHHHHHHHHHHHHHHHHHHHH!" the girl screamed in utter humiliation.

Everyone immediately burst out in laughter, including Daniel. However, because he was not paying attention, he was unaware of Myles slowly sneaking up towards him. While Daniel was busy sharing a laugh with the rest of the cafeteria, Myles pulled his arm back and threw the slice of cake he had in his hand at Daniel.

SPLAT!

Daniel was stunned after being hit in the face with that cake. Myles instantly laughed. However, a hush began to take over the cafeteria as everyone looked over at Daniel as some of the cake residue began to fall from his face. Daniel looked over at Myles with fire in his eyes. Before Daniel could take his first step to retaliate, one of the basketball players stood on the table and before anyone knew it, he yelled out, ***"FOOD FIGHT!"***

Immediately, everyone began to pick up any article of food they could find, and they started throwing it. It did not matter who was hit. Everyone had targets on their backs. It was a big catastrophe. Food was flying everywhere as this huge warzone ensued.

FWEEEEEET!

Everyone stopped in their tracks; however, before Principal Lawson could continue, *SPLAT!*

The entire cafeteria gasped after watching Principal Lawson being hit with a big piece of cake. It was as if time stood still. After a few more seconds, Principal Lawson furiously wiped the cake off his face. Then, he looked around at everyone and the horrible mess that was right in front of him. "WHO STARTED THIS FOOD FIGHT?

AND I WANT ANSWERS RIGHT NOW!" Principal Lawson yelled.

Everyone immediately pointed at either Daniel, Brittany, or Myles.

"YOU THREE!" Principal Lawson bellowed. "COME WITH ME! RIGHT NOW!"

Daniel, Brittany, and Myles slowly walked towards Principal Lawson.

"And now I want the rest of you to clean up this mess before the next bell rings!" Principal Lawson proclaimed to the rest of the students in the rest of the cafeteria, but no one moved. It was as if they were still frozen with fear.... or just in sheer shock of it all. However, Principal Lawson quickly snapped them back into reality and shouted, "NOW!!!!!!!!!"

The students quickly moved and began to clean up the cafeteria as Principal Lawson walked Daniel, Brittany, and Myles out of the cafeteria.

Back at the Emblem Validation Insignia Licensing Manufacturing Company, hundreds of male laborers, each wearing black shades around their eye socket, were working hard operating the huge manufacturing machines mass-producing hundreds and hundreds of identification badges. While the assembly line workers were operating the machines, one worker, who was also wearing black shades, was sitting at the computer inputting names and pictures into the system. Suddenly, these names began to appear on the screen:

DANIEL RICHARDS

BRITTANY KNOWLES

NAOMI LAWSON

DIERDRE CLAYTON

JARED TAYLOR

MYLES TAYLOR

Other workers removed the completed ID badges and placed metal magnets on the connectors of the lanyards. Suddenly, the metal magnets began to glow with red letters of on them: E.V.I.L.

CHAPTER SIX

The door creaked open, and Principal Lawson, Myles, Brittany, and Daniel began to walk down the stairs. Principal Lawson kept a stern and stoic countenance as he wiped the remaining residue of cake off his face while Myles, Brittany, and Daniel looked at their current surroundings with fear and concern looks on their faces.

"Principal Lawson," Daniel began, "where are you taking us?"

"To our new in-house suspension facility," Principal Lawson grimly responded.

"Downstairs?" Myles wondered.

"I never knew we had an in-house suspension facility," Brittany interjected.

"I didn't even know we had a downstairs," Daniel jokingly added.

However, no one seemed to laugh as they continued to make their way down the dark and cold stairwell.

“Well, we do now... and you all are the first ones to try it out,” Principal Lawson agitatedly responded as they made to the bottom of the stairs, which seemed to take longer than eternity.

Principal Lawson reached for the doorknob and tried to turn it, but it appeared to be stuck.

Brittany, Myles, and Daniel noticed that Principal Lawson was having a problem opening the door.

“You alright, Principal Lawson?” Myles asked.

“Look like you are struggling a little bit,” Daniel added.

“Would you be quiet?” Principal Lawson shouted. Then, he continued to attempt to get the door open. “Maybe if you would stop talking, I could get... this... door.... open!”

Finally, the door opened after Principal Lawson’s last forceful push. Then, Principal Lawson looked at Brittany, Myles, and Daniel with what looked like a sinister smile and said, “Welcome to your new home until the end of the school day.”

With fear coursing through their veins, Myles, Brittany, and Daniel slowly walked into the old, abandoned classroom, which appeared to be covered in dust and cobwebs.

Myles looked and saw his little brother sitting in one of the desks along with Naomi and Deek. "Jared?" Myles wondered.

"Have a seat," Principal Lawson ordered.

Myles, Brittany, and Daniel sat down joining Jared, Naomi, and Deek in what equated to what a prison would look and feel like in their adolescent minds.

"Now, I'll be back to get you when the final bell rings," Principal Lawson bellowed. "You are to take this time to think about what you've done, and how you are going to resolve the bad decisions each of you have made. A teacher will be down here shortly to monitor you for the rest of the day. I am ashamed and disappointed in each and every one of you."

However, Principal Lawson sternly glared at Naomi as he ended his lecture. Naomi held her head down in shame and sadness as Principal Lawson walked out of the room and slammed the door behind him.

Chaos and confusion continued to consume the front office as different people were either entering and exiting or coming and going. Principal Lawson entered trying to get through all the utter madness that ensued. Kim could see the exasperation and frustration on Principal Lawson's face as she made her way through the horde to get to him. "Principal Lawson, are you okay?" she asked.

"Ask me that when I retire," Principal Lawson gravely answered.

"Well, you have someone waiting for you in your office," Kim cheerfully said trying to shift the negative energy that was astoundingly present.

"Gee. Thanks," Principal Lawson sarcastically responded as he walked to his office door, opened it, and walked in his office closing the door behind him.

Kim sighed. *I hope things get better around here soon,* she optimistically hoped in her head.

Meanwhile, in Principal Lawson's office, Principal Lawson was confused to why his chair was turned away from him. It was apparent that someone else was sitting in it. "Excuse you," he began with an appalled tone in his voice.

Suddenly, the chair turned around revealing Mr. Malo occupying the throne.

"Mr. Malo," Principal Lawson responded as a sudden looming fear began to fill the room and Principal Lawson's heart.

"The ID badges are here and are ready to be passed out to your students and the faculty, Principal Lawson," Mr. Malo stated.

"Man, that was quick."

"I told you. We provide quality, *fast* service."

"Great," Principal Lawson nervously smiled and said. Then, he looked around and asked, "So... where are the badges?"

"My workmen are hand delivering them to every single classroom right now."

Immediately, the next bell began to ring.

Then, Mr. Malo mischievously smirked. "Right on cue. It's showtime!"

In the hallway, several men and women in all black suits with black shades covering their eyes marched down the hallway, and each of them were carrying a box of ID badges. They each began to separate from the pack as they approached their assigned classrooms. Then, the workers each opened a door and entered.

"Now, you'll remember there are three types of angles: the acute, the right, and the obtuse," the geometry teacher said in his classroom. However, his lesson was interrupted as she noticed her door was opened and one of the workers walked in carrying a box of badges.

"Excuse you? Who are you and what are you doing here?" the teacher confusedly asked.

"These are the new ID badges that Principal Lawson ordered from our company for the faculty and students," the worker plainly stated.

"ID badges?" the teacher wondered with an even more confused look on her face. "When did this happen?"

"Today," the worker firmly retorted. "Now, I will begin to hand out your IDs."

The worker put the box on the desk and opened it. Then, the worker began pulling out the IDs and passing them out calling each person by their last name. "Anderson... Attaway... Bloomington... Blount..."

Each student as they were called walked up to receive their ID badges with bewildered expressions on their faces. However, the roll call went this way in each and every classroom.

"Burke... Carrington... Clay... Cox... Davis..."

"Dell... Dixon... Dunwoody... Ellis..."

Back in the front office, Principal Lawson watched as Mr. Malo passed out ID badges to all the administrative staff. Then, Mr. Malo turned to Principal Lawson and handed him one. "Here's yours," Principal Lawson assuredly said with a sly smile on his face.

"Thank you," Principal Lawson replied as he was about to put the lanyard around neck, but Mr. Malo swiftly stopped him.

"Not yet!"

Principal Lawson looked at him with perplexity all over his face.

"Please wait until everyone in the school has theirs," Mr. Malo instructed. "I want everyone to put them on together. Unity, right?"

"Right," Principal Lawson nervously responded not knowing that what was about to happen next would change the course of everything.

Daniel, Brittany, Myles, Jared, Naomi, and Deek continued to sit quietly in their seats in the hoary and grimy room being used as the "new" in-house suspension facility.

Brittany started looking around at the cold décor, but suddenly, a big cockroach scattered across the floor.

"Eeek!" Brittany shrilled.

Everyone else looked at her trying to figure out what was going on.

"Yuck!" she continued. "We have got to get out of here."

"It's only been a few minutes," Daniel teased.

"I wonder what's going on up there in the real world," Jared said.

"The real world sucks," Deek interjected.

"I'm sure your world does, *freak*," Daniel rudely insinuated.

Deek scoffed and rolled her eyes as Myles shook his head in disgust at the insult that Daniel hurled at her.

"Daniel, why do you always have to be so mean?" Brittany wondered.

"And why do you always have to be so nice?" Daniel retorted.

"Deflection," Myles said under his breath.

"So, you don't believe in peace and being kind to others?" Brittany challenged Daniel.

"Oh, you definitely didn't believe in it when you slammed that cake in that girl's face!" Daniel exclaimed. "What ever happened to 'increase the peace?'"

"It went out the window when you purposely flirted with that girl, and she put her nasty lips on you!"

"No different than you talking to dudes that I forbid you to talk to!"

"Forbid me?" Brittany shouted. "You can't forbid me to do anything! You are not my father!"

Myles, Jared, Naomi, and Deek watched as Brittany and Daniel continued to argue. As things began to escalate, Myles turned to his little brother and asked, "So.... how did you end up here?"

"I skipped class," Jared admitted. "Well... try a few classes with her."

Myles looked over at Naomi after his brother gestured in her direction. "Come on, Jared," he said to his sibling, "You can't be hanging with the wrong crowd."

"I thought you weren't going to be looking out for me anymore," Jared stated reminding his older brother of what he said.

"I wouldn't have to look out for you all the time if you would stop getting in trouble."

"And what about you? Huh? What are you doing here?"

"Ask that jerk over there!" Myles exclaimed pointing to Daniel.

Daniel realized that Myles was referring to him as he turned his attention away from Brittany, stood up, and ran up on Myles. "Excuse me, punk!" he contested. "If you got something to say, then say it to my face!"

Myles stood up and responded, "No problem... PUNK!"

Myles and Daniel began to square off, but Brittany and Jared quickly jumped in order to prevent an even bigger melee. Naomi continued to observe the atrocity that was in front of her. "This is all a mess," she said.

"Well... this is all your daddy's fault, *princess*," Deek responded. "He's the one that came up with this dumb in-house suspension mess."

"Don't be talking about my daddy, you low-class freak," Naomi insulted.

And just like that, Naomi and Deek began to go back and forth with each other joining the ruckus. Unbeknown to them, the classroom door slowly began to open, and Michael walked in. He looked around him, and to his dismay, he witnessed the chaos and calamity that was before him. He shook his head with shame, but suddenly, he slammed the door closed. Everyone immediately stopped arguing and fussing, and they looked at Michael.

"Hello all!" Michael cheerfully greeted. "I'm Michael... and I'm your in-house suspension teacher. Please take your seats."

Michael smiled, and it was as if a glimmer of light and hope began to enter the room shifting the atmosphere. Daniel, Myles, Brittany, Jared, Naomi, and Deek took their seats as Michael slowly and calmly walked to the front of the room. "Now," he began, "what seems to be the problem here?"

"No problem. It's just that I can't stand that PUNK over there," Daniel replied referring to Myles.

"Trust me," Myles responded. "The feeling is mutual."

"First off, can we not resort to the name calling?" Michael requested. "Secondly, Daniel, how can you be a good leader if you can't get along with your teammate?"

"Teammate?" Daniel scoffed. "I ain't on a team with *him*!"

"And best believe there ain't a team in the world that anyone would want to be on if you're on it!" Myles countered. "Besides, I don't follow. I lead."

"Humility is the key to being a quality leader," Michael recounted.

"Being peaceful is also a quality, too," Brittany inserted. "Right, Michael?"

"Yes," Michael replied. "But we must also practice what we preach."

Feeling hit, Brittany slowly lowered her head.

"Listen," Naomi interjected, "if we're all done with this morality lesson---"

"Are you sure you're done?" Michael challenged.

"I'm sure," Naomi responded. "I'm good. In fact... I'm perfectly fine."

"Looks like you're still struggling with the truth, huh?" Michael questioned causing Naomi to truly re-examine what she previously stated.

"Yo! What's your beef, man?" Deek exclaimed.

"What's yours, Deirdre?" Michael asked.

"That's Deek," she firmly stated correcting Michael.

"Why are you so bitter and so apathetic towards life?" Michael wondered.

"Why shouldn't I be?" Deek replied. "Life has dealt me a bad hand."

"Life is what you make it," Michael responded. "You can choose your destiny and having a positive attitude can help you make the right choice."

"What I need is salvation from this life," Deek grimly mumbled.

Michael sighed with sadness at Deek's response. Then, he looked over at Jared, who was silently sitting in his seat as if he was invisible to the world. "Jared, do you have anything to say?" Michael asked him.

Jared looked up at Michael, who had a glimmer of hope in his eye. But then, Jared looked away and quietly said, "No."

"You have a voice, Jared," Michael said trying to reassure him. "Use it."

"Why should I?" Jared responded. "Nobody wants to listen to me anyway."

Michael sighed again watching Jared lower his head as if he had no confidence at all. Michael slowly began to approach Jared, and he lightly lifted Jared's head with his hand making direct eye contact with him. "You need to have faith in yourself," Michael assertively stated yet in a loving and gentle manner. "You are valuable and important."

Jared could see the glimmer in Michael's eyes as Michael spoke life into him and stirring up hope and reassurance inside of him. Michael walked away from Jared and returned to the front of the classroom looking at all of them with the same glimmer of hope. "All of you are valuable and important, and you have to realize that," Michael continued. "But you can't realize it until you all quit all this bickering and backbiting and work together. The fate of the world is depended on you."

The room felt like it came to a sudden halt after Michael's last statement as the teenagers each looked at one another with confused and puzzled expressions on their faces.

"The fate of the world?" Brittany wondered.

"What does all of us getting along and working together have to do with the world?" Myles asked.

Michael then cleared his throat. "Come on, you all," he said quickly changing the subject.

"Where are we going?" Naomi asked.

"We're going somewhere that will teach you all how to work together as a team," Michael answered.

“Do we have to?” Deek challenged.

“Either you can go and do something constructive,” Michael responded, “or you can sit in this room... with each other... in silence... until the end of the day.”

Deek, Naomi, Jared, Myles, Brittany, and Daniel looked at one another exchanging glances. Then, they turned to Michael and said, “Let’s go!”

The teens each got up from their seats as Michael opened the door, and they walked out of the classroom. However, Daniel, being the last one to leave, stopped in front of Michael. “Learning to work together as a team, huh?” he asked.

“Learning to work together as a team,” Michael repeated with reassurance.

Then, Daniel walked out of the door. “Trust me,” Michael said out loud to himself. “You all are going to need it.”

Suddenly, that gold twinkle brightly lit up in Michael’s eyes, and he walked out the door closing it behind him.

Meanwhile, back at the front office of the school, Mr. Malo looked at his watch and said, “Everyone should have their badges by now." Then, he turned to Principal Lawson and asked, "May I use your intercom?"

"Well, actually, I'm the only one who uses the intercom," Principal Lawson said.

"Please, Principal Lawson," Mr. Malo smoothly and persuasively retorted. "This is a special occasion, and I want you to share in it."

"Fine," Principal Lawson responded with a sigh. "I guess."

"Excellent," Mr. Malo said with a sinister grin. Then, he walked over to the intercom and pressed the button. "Hello, students and faculty of Rowlands High School! I am Mr. Malo, the CEO of the Emblem Validation Insignia Licensing Manufacturing Company, and I hope you all have your IDs and will enjoy wearing them. And now... this is the moment you've all been waiting for. You may now... put on your ID badges."

Following Mr. Malo's instructions, Principal Lawson, Kim, and the other staff members put the lanyards around their necks, and suddenly, the metal magnets attached themselves to the back of their necks. As soon as that happened, their eye sockets immediately turned red. Mr. Malo looked around and ominously cackled at his creation. Suddenly, Mr. Malo began to roar loudly shedding and breaking out of his human skin revealing his true form as Nefarious. Then, Nefarious pressed the intercom button and commanded in his snarly, vile voice, "Now... I want all of you to search this entire building for the six crosses... AND BRING THEM TO ME!"

Immediately, each and every student and teacher from every classroom — all of them with red eyeball sockets — rushed out of the classrooms creating chaos and calamity in the hallways as they obeyed Nefarious' orders. Then, the men and women in business suits yelled just as furiously as Nefarious, and they broke out of their uniforms and human skin revealing their true nature as evil horsemen following suit after their master.

Nefarious watched as the possessed Principal Lawson and the rest of the faculty and staff stormed out of the office. Then, Nefarious picked up the intercom and crushed it with his bare hands maliciously laughing as the dark smoke exuded from his body. "And now.... IT'S SHOWTIME!"

CHAPTER SEVEN

Down in the deep, dark, and damp basement, Daniel, Brittany, Myles, Jared, Deek, and Naomi were quietly and begrudgingly cleaning up.

Daniel sighed aggravatedly breaking the silence. "I don't see how cleaning up this basement is going to help us to 'work together,'" he stated with sarcasm.

"Just shut up and clean," Myles instantly snapped.

"Don't start nothing, won't be nothing," Daniel quickly responded as he began to spar up against his nemesis.

"Please, guys! Let's just clean," Brittany protested trying to prevent Daniel and Myles from getting into another argument. "The faster we clean, the faster we can get out of here."

"Look, Michael, I've had a change of heart. Can we..." Naomi said with frustration as she looked around, but then, she realized that Michael was not in the room with them. "Where is Michael?"

Everyone else began to look around them finally realizing that Michael was nowhere to be found.

"Figures he would leave us to do all the work," Deek scoffed as she walked away from the group and sat in the corner by herself.

Jared looked and saw Deek sitting alone. Then, he sighed and began to walk over to her while Daniel, Brittany, Myles, and Naomi continued to unwillingly clean up the messy basement.

Deek grumbled to herself, but after a few seconds, she looked up to see Jared walking over to her with a smile on his face.

"What do you want?" Deek said with a sullen expression.

"I'm sorry that life sucks for you," Jared sincerely said as he sat down beside her.

"Awww, gee. Thanks," Deek said in a sarcastic tone.

Jared sighed as he tried to collect the right words to say. He could see that Deek was hurting, and he wanted to make sure that what he said next would help rather than hinder. "The thing is," he began. "I definitely know how you feel."

Deek gave Jared a look that could freeze the entire city. *How could you know how I feel, new kid?*

"I've always been under the shadow of my brother," Jared continued. "He has always been popular, better at sports, better at school, better with the girls. We had to move here to Garden City from L.A. because my dad got a new job. I mean, even though my life sucks, at least I was somewhere familiar with people my age who understood and actually liked me. My parents are always so proud of Myles. They're even proud of the way he's handling the situation of moving here. Just once... I would want for them to be as proud of me as they are of Myles."

"Oh, please!" Deek exclaimed as her frustration began to mutate into anger. "You think that's bad? At least you have a brother! At least you have a mom and dad! I don't have a mother, or a father, or a brother.... I am an orphan! I don't even know who my family is! My parents abandoned me and left me alone to die! And if you think your life sucks, then you need to look in a mirror really quickly and re-evaluate it because I would trade places with you in a heartbeat!"

Jared looked at Deek and could see the angry expression on her face, but most importantly, he looked deeply and could see the hurt and pain in her eyes. "You're right," he responded. "I'm sorry."

Deek did not say anything as she looked away as if she was a little embarrassed by her sudden outburst.

"Listen," Jared resumed. "I know that you think life is unfair... and you have every right to. But just have faith in God. He'll get you through the rough times."

"Faith in God?" Deek wondered. Then, she immediately dismissed the thought and scoffed, "Please! If there is a God, why would He allow all these bad things to happen to me?"

"I don't know," Jared admittedly replied. "You mentioned to Michael that you needed salvation from this life---"

"Yeah... so?" Deek interrupted.

Jared sighed and continued, "'For God so loved the world that He gave his only begotten Son, but whosoever believeth in Him shall not perish but have everlasting life.'"

"What is that supposed to mean?" Deek instantaneously challenged.

"Jesus is the salvation you need," Jared kindly explained, "and He's the one that is going to get you through his life and make it better."

"Yeah... right," Deek responded with snark.

"And if you don't remember anything else, remember this," Jared said as he lightly touched Deek on her shoulder with comfort, "God loves you."

Jared stood up and walked away. Deek sat there in disbelief. *It's nice that someone seems to actually care about me*, she thought as a smile began to appear on her face. Suddenly, she started to realize what was happening, and she quickly stopped smiling before anybody could see her.

Suddenly, a loud rumbling could be heard from upstairs.

"Do y'all hear that?" Myles wondered.

"It sounds like a lot of noise from upstairs in the school," Brittany said.

"I wonder what's going on," Naomi chimed in.

"Let's go find out," Daniel suggested.

"But what about the rest of this mess?" Jared innocently asked.

"Forget the mess," Naomi responded. "Something could be terribly wrong."

"You heard the lady. Let's go," Daniel ordered as he along with Brittany, Myles, Jared, Naomi, and Deek rushed up the stairs exiting the basement.

Meanwhile, in the front office, files and documents were everywhere while copy machines and desks were turned over as a possessed Principal Lawson along with the faculty members were frantically searching for those crosses. Suddenly, the door swung open, and one of the horsemen walked into the office and bypassed all the possessed people as he walked into Principal Lawson's office, where the door had been torn off its hinges.

The horsemen entered Principal Lawson's office to Nefarious sitting in Lawson's chair. The horsemen pulled out six ID badges from his pouch. "Nefarious, it has been reported that these six students are not wearing their badges," the horseman stated.

"Then find them!" Nefarious vilely shouted. "The prophecy says that the keepers of the crosses are youth. We cannot let that prophecy come to pass!"

"Nefarious," the horseman explained, "the school

has been searched from top to bottom. There are no crosses."

"SILENCE!" Nefarious yelled with smoke coming from his pores. "Michael was here! If Michael was here that means those crosses have to be here! And we ain't going anywhere until we find them. Now... FIND THEM!"

Daniel, Brittany, Myles, Naomi, Jared, and Deek walked down the hallway with shocked and confused expressions on their faces as they saw that everything was in disarray. They watched in horror as their classmates and teachers ripped off the doors from the lockers frantically searching for something as if their lives depended on it.

"What is going on here? What is the matter with everyone?" Brittany worriedly asked.

"I don't know. It's as if this whole school has gone amuck," Daniel said.

"My daddy is going to have a field day," Naomi added.

Myles looked to see a student rummaging through his things at his locker. Then, he stormed over to him and shouted, "Hey! What are you doing in my locker?"

Suddenly, the student turned around and growled at Myles revealing his red eye sockets. Myles jumped back in fear and rushed back to the others. Then, Myles, Daniel, Brittany, Naomi, Jared, and Deek looked around and observed what was happening with everyone else around them.

"All of their eyes," Myles began.

"...are red!" Jared screamed.

"There's something freaky going on around here," Deek objected.

"HEY! YOU KIDS!"

Myles, Daniel, Brittany, Naomi, Jared, and Deek turned around to see one of the horsemen approaching them.

"AHHHHHHHHHHHHHHHHHHHHHHHHHHHHH!" both Brittany and Naomi screamed with horrified looks on their faces.

"What the---" Daniel said not really knowing how to react to the horrible creature coming towards them.

"GET BACK TO WORK!" the horseman bellowed.

"To work?" Daniel asked with confusion. "What work? Who are you?"

"What are you?" Myles interjected.

Suddenly, the front office door opened, and the horseman with the ID badges entered the hallway.

"It seems that we have some insubordinates," the second horseman said to the head horseman.

The head horseman looked over at Brittany, Daniel, Myles, Jared, Naomi, and Deek. "That's because they aren't wearing *these* badges," he responded, "and we don't have them under our control."

"I knew something freaky was going on!" Deek exclaimed.

"COME HERE!" the head horseman roared.

"Run!" Myles shouted.

Immediately, Myles, Daniel, Brittany, Jared, Deek, and Naomi ran for their lives through all the crowds of chaos. The head horseman snapped his fingers and ordered, "AFTER THEM!"

Suddenly, the mind-controlled students and faculty stopped tearing up the lockers in search for the crosses, and they began to chase after Myles, Daniel, Brittany, Jared, Deek, and Naomi. As the young escapees continued to run down another part of the hallway, which was a total catastrophe of papers, books, and knocked-down lockers everywhere, suddenly, a hand from a classroom reached out and grabbed Britany's foot causing her to fall to the floor.

"AHHHHHHHHHHHHHHH!" Brittany frantically screamed as she turned around to see several students with glowing red eyeball sockets standing over her and growling as if they are ready to devour every inch of her body.

Suddenly, Daniel and Myles rushed to Brittany's rescue. Daniel started forcibly pushing the possessed students away while Myles helped Brittany up off the floor, and Myles and Brittany began to run away to rejoin the others. However, as Daniel started to escape with them, a horseman appeared and grabbed Daniel from behind bearhugging him.

"Let go of me!" Daniel protested.

The horseman then pulled out a small device from his pouch and placed it on Daniel's back. Then, the horseman continued squeezing Daniel tightly as if to try to crush all the life force from his teenage body. "HELPPPPPPPPPPPP!" he desperately yelled.

Brittany and Myles turned around to see Daniel being held captive by the evil horseman.

"Oh no!" Brittany exclaimed. "He has Daniel!"

"You go catch up with the rest of them," Myles instructed. "I'll get Daniel."

However, Brittany did not move. She was stuck with fear gluing her feet to the floor.

"GO!" Myles yelled snapping Brittany out of her own fearful paralysis.

Brittany quickly ran away as Myles rushed towards the horseman and Daniel. As soon as Daniel approached the horseman, he grabbed the evil creature by the arm and tried to loosen his grip on Daniel. However, the horseman proved to be too strong and too powerful for the young lad, and suddenly, the horseman backslapped Myles causing him to fly into the lockers and land forcibly on the floor knocking him out immediately.

"Myles!" Daniel called out.

However, Daniel realized that the horseman's grip was not as tight as before causing Daniel to have room to maneuver. So, Daniel quickly elbowed the horseman in the stomach with all his might, which knocked the wind out of the horseman causing him to release Daniel. Daniel immediately turned around and roundhouse kicked the horseman in the chest knocking him down to the floor. Then, Daniel ran towards Myles, who was still knocked out. Daniel kneeled and began to try and wake Myles up. "Come on, Myles. We gotta go. C'mon, man. Wake up. Wake up!"

Suddenly, Daniel looked up to see a mind-controlled crowd of students and faculty members running down the hallway towards them. Frantically, Daniel began slapping Myles in the face to wake him up. "Wake up, Myles! We gotta go! Wake up, man!

Daniel began to lift Myles up as Myles started to come to. "What's going on?" Myles asked with confusion.

"C'mon, man! We gotta go!" Daniel warned as he put Myles' arm around his neck, and they quickly ran down the hallway as the possessed mob chased after them.

In the meantime, Deek, Naomi, Jared, and Brittany continued to run down the stairs towards the lower level of the school. "Are they after us?" Naomi wondered.

"I don't know!" Jared responded. "Let's just keep running!"

Brittany turned around, and she smiled happily after seeing that Daniel and Myles had caught up to them.

"I think I got it from here," Myles said. "Thanks."

"Don't mention it," Daniel responded as they both began to run down the stairs.

Deek, Naomi, Jared, and Brittany quickly ran into the basement, but then, they realized that may not have been the best idea. "Oh, my goodness!" Naomi shouted. "Why did we come down here?"

"We're trapped!" Brittany screamed.

"I'm sorry! I don't think well under pressure!" Jared retorted.

Then, Daniel and Myles ran into the basement finally catching up with the rest of the team. "Quick, Jared," Daniel called out, "help me close this door! They're coming!"

Jared rushed over to Daniel, and they both pushed the door closed. As Myles moved to the middle of the basement trying to get better control of his breathing, Daniel locked the door. "That ought to hold them," Daniel said with assurance hoping it would give them time to think of a plan to escape.

However, there was a loud pounding. The group of worried teens looked at the door to see the crowd of possessed students and teachers banging and pushing against the door from the outside. Daniel and Jared then rushed to the door and pressed their bodies against it trying to prevent it from bursting open. “Never mind,” Daniel responded.

“We have to get out of here!” Brittany exclaimed.

“There has to be some way out of here,” Myles said in a calming manner.

“Naomi, can you think of anything?” Jared asked.

“I don’t know,” Naomi replied. “I’ve never actually been down here in the basement before today.”

“We’re doomed!” Deek shouted with despair.

“Don’t say that!” Jared yelled back.

“The reality is until we find a way out of here and get past all of those possessed people and those scary creatures... WE... ARE... DOOMED!” Deek countered.

Suddenly, the pounding and slamming against the door continued as Jared and Daniel could feel their weight against the door becoming lighter by the second. “We’re going to have to do something because I don’t know how long we’re going to be able to hold this door,” Daniel said.

“Looks like we’re going to have to fight our way through,” Myles said. “Everyone grab something!”

Brittany, Naomi, Deek, and Myles began to look around for an object to grab. As everyone frantically searched, Daniel looked to see Myles walking over to the bookshelf. "A book?" Daniel wondered. "How are you going to fight with a book?"

"Just keep the door closed!" Myles shouted back.

Myles continued to look throughout the bookshelf, but then, suddenly, something caught his eye: a large, gold book. *What in the world is this?*

The enticement of the book continued to captivate him as he slowly began to reach for it. Myles slowly touched the book and pulled it towards him. Suddenly, rumbling began to take over the entire space. Everyone looked around with worried looks on their faces as one of the walls began to open up. "Oh, wow!" Myles exclaimed.

"A secret passage," Brittany said.

"Where does it lead?" Naomi wondered.

"Who cares! Let's get the heck out of here!" Deek shouted.

"But what about us?" Jared frighteningly asked.

"We'll run first, and then, once we're in the clear, y'all come on down, and Jared, you push the book back, so they won't follow us," Myles instructed.

"But..." Jared began to protest.

"Just have faith," Myles said trying to reassure his little brother.

Suddenly, a hand punched through the door trying to grab Daniel and Jared. Then, several other hands began to punch through the door. "Run!" Daniel yelled.

Brittany, Naomi, Deek, and Myles immediately began to run through the secret passage.

"Let's go!" Daniel said to Jared.

Then, Jared and Daniel moved away from the door and rushed over to the wall. Suddenly, the crowd of possessed students and faculty members burst through the door; however, they struggled to get through the entrance because the door was too narrow, and everyone was trying to fight their way through. Seeing that this was their opportunity to escape, Daniel ran through the secret passage. Jared quickly pushed the golden book back in its original position, and suddenly, the wall began to close. Jared gulped with fear. *What if I don't make it? What's going to happen to me?*

However, despite his fearful thoughts, Jared took a deep breath and then, hurriedly slid through the secret passage seconds before the wall closed shut.

CHAPTER EIGHT

"THEY WHAT?!" Nefarious angrily bellowed as smoke began to fill Principal Lawson's office.

The head horseman stood there with nervousness as Nefarious huffed and puffed in his face. "They.... they... they escaped, Nefarious," he finally said.

"YOU FOOL!" Nefarious screamed. "WHY DID YOU LET THEM ESCAPE?"

"I... I... I don't know, your majesty," the head horseman said. Then, he bowed and apologized, "I'm sorry."

"You definitely are!" Nefarious responded. "Now, get up!"

The head horseman slowly stood up. "But your majesty... when one of those kids were almost captured, one of the horsemen managed to accidentally attach a tracking device to him."

"Really?" Nefarious responded with a sinister smile on his face.

The horseman pulled out a tracker, and on the screen, there is a small light moving on the screen. "It seems that they are in a hidden chamber somewhere located in the school. Should we go after them, sire?"

"No," Nefarious answered with a snarl. "Let's just see where they go. They may lead us to those crosses."

The small tracking device on Daniel's back continued to quietly emit the radio frequency signal as he, along with Myles, Jared, Naomi, Deek, and Brittany, slowly made their way through the dark chamber. The flames of light hanging on the chamber walls guided the teenagers as they continued to look around trying to figure out exactly where they were going.

"Does anyone know where we are and where we're going?" Deek asked.

"As long as we are away from those ugly creatures, then, I don't care where we are," Naomi honestly responded.

Brittany turned to Myles and asked, "Are you scared?"

Yes, I'm terrified, Myles immediately thought, but he knew that he could not say that out loud. He had to continue to exude confidence amongst the group. "Um.... no.... not really," he finally responded. "Listen, everyone, let's just make sure we all stick close together, so we don't get lost."

The group of brave teenagers continued down the path of the dark chamber; however, they suddenly stopped as they came along a pathway that leads in four different directions.

"Uh oh," Brittany said.

"Where do we go from here?" Daniel wondered.

"I have no earthly idea," Myles said.

"Well, we need to make a decision," Naomi responded. "It's only a matter of time before those ug-mugs come after us!"

"Maybe we should split up," Daniel suggested.

"No," Myles immediately recanted. "Bad idea."

"So... what do we do, Myles?" Jared asked.

Myles sighed, and then, he answered, "Let's just take a moment to re-group so that we make a wise decision."

After Myles said that Deek walked over to a section by herself. Then, Brittany walked over to Daniel while Jared joined Myles and Naomi.

"Hey," Brittany said.

"Hey. How are you holding up?" Daniel asked.

"Barely. You?"

"I'm still a little injured from that bear hug that — whatever the heck that thing was — gave me."

"You know... if it wasn't for Myles, you wouldn't have gotten out of there."

She's right, Daniel thought, but there was no way that he would admit that out loud.

"It looks like you two can work together after all," Brittany added.

Daniel sighed heavily.

Meanwhile, Naomi playfully pushed Jared. "Hey," she said. "Good work back there."

"Thanks. I didn't think I could do it," Jared admitted.

"I knew you could," Naomi said.

"So did I," Myles interjected.

Jared bashfully smiled and said, "Thanks."

"See what a little faith can do," Myles said smiling back.

Naomi smiled as well and then slowly walked away.

"I'm glad you're leading us, Myles," Jared said to his older brother. "I don't know what we'd do without you."

"Can I be honest with you?" Myles asked.

"Sure."

"Remember when Brittany asked me, 'Was I scared?'"

"Yeah?"

"I've been scared out of my mind this entire time."

"That's what makes a great leader," Jared responded with encouragement. "Even though you're scared, none of us realize it. And you're keeping it together so well that it's keeping all of us together."

"Thanks, little brother," Myles said. "I needed to hear that."

"You're welcome. I'm always here for you when you need me."

"Same here," Myles said with reassurance as he grabbed Jared and hugged him tightly. "Always."

While hugging his brother, Myles looked up and saw Brittany walking over to Deek.

"Hey, Deek," Brittany politely greeted. "How are you holding up?"

"Do you really care?" Deek asked with snark.

"I wouldn't ask if I didn't," Brittany sassily responded.

"Answer this for me. If we weren't in this situation, would you even be talking to me? Would you even be saying one word to me?"

Brittany shrugged her shoulders and sighed. "Probably not," she honestly answered. "But the point is that we are, and I am. We all have to remember that we are all in this together. We all need to work together if we're going to get out of this mess alive."

Deek sighed, and then, Brittany looked over to see Daniel approaching Myles and Jared. Brittany slightly smiled hoping that this next interaction would be a positive one.

"Hey," Daniel said to Myles.

"Hey," Myles responded.

Jared noticed the awkward silence between the two alpha males. "I'ma let you two... talk," he said as he slowly walked away.

After a few more seconds, Daniel finally continued. "I just wanted to say... thank you."

"For what?" Myles asked.

"For coming back to rescue me from that... that thing. You could've just left me to fend for myself, but you didn't."

"And thank you for saving me when that monster knocked me out."

"No problem."

After the admission of thankfulness, there was another passage of uncomfortable silence between the two of them.

"I still don't appreciate you messing with my girl," Daniel blurted out.

"And I still don't appreciate you acting like a pompous jerk," Myles retorted.

Myles and Daniel then glared at each other, but then, their glares turned into light smiles. Daniel held his hand out towards Myles. "Truce?"

Myles studied Daniel's hand. Then, he sighed and hesitantly returned the favor by shaking Daniel's hand in agreement. "Truce."

Suddenly, a small light began to illuminate from the upper left chamber column.

"What is that?" Daniel asked noticing the radiant glow.

Myles turned around and was mesmerized by the illumination. "I don't know," he responded.

Brittany, Deek, Naomi, and Jared slowly joined Myles and Daniel as they stared into the light. "I wonder where it leads," Brittany said.

"I guess we should find out," Myles suggested. "Let's go. But remember... stick close together."

Everyone nodded their heads in agreement as they slowly walked towards the upper left chamber column, and they bravely entered the unknown one by one.

The valiant group of six continued down the chamber following the illumination that guided their wondering footsteps. "The light is getting more and more intense," Myles stated. "This is probably the right direction."

As Myles continued leading the group, he placed his foot down on an unstable part of the ground, and suddenly, the ground crumbled right from beneath his foot causing him to fall, but Daniel quickly grabbed Myles by one of his arms. Brittany, Naomi, Deek, and Jared gasped with terror as they saw the gigantic hole in the ground that appeared to be about a few feet wide and infinite amount of feet in depth. "AHHHHHHHHHHHHHH!" Myles screamed as his feet dangled over the hole.

"Don't worry, Myles. I got you," Daniel said trying to hold him up with all of his strength and might.

"Don't let me go!" Myles begged.

"I won't let you go!" Daniel reassured him.

"What do we do?" Brittany asked.

Jared hurriedly ran over and kneeled. "Myles, give me your other arm."

"Jared, no! Back away!" Myles ordered. "I don't want you to fall!"

"Give me your other arm, Myles!" Jared countered. "Now!"

"No!" Myles shouted wishing that his little brother would just listen to him.

"Have faith in me, Myles," Jared pleaded. "Now, please, give me your other arm!"

Myles sighed realizing that he had no other choice. Then, with all his power, Myles slung his other arm, and Jared caught it.

"Myles, we're going to need your help in getting you up, okay," Daniel instructed.

"Okay."

"On three," Daniel said. "One... two... three!"

Daniel and Jared began to pull Myles up as Myles struggled to help them by using his legs to push against the rocks. Watching Jared and Daniel trying to pull Myles up, Brittany looked at Naomi and Deek, and it appeared that all three of them had the same idea as they all rushed over and grabbed Daniel and Jared as they all pulled Myles up from falling to his doom. After a full more tugs, they successfully pulled Myles up causing them all to fall to the ground. They all sighed with relief after working together to save Myles. After catching their breath, they each stood up. "Oh, thank God, you're safe!" Brittany said.

"Thank you," Myles responded. "Thank all of you."

Then, Myles looked over to his little brother, and then, he rushed over and hugged him. “Thank you, little brother.”

“No problem. I told you I’m always here for you,” Jared happily said.

Then, Myles hugged Deek, Naomi, and Brittany. Finally, Myles turned over to Daniel as if he was about to hug him, but Daniel immediately stopped him. “No need for the hugs. Your gratitude is good enough.”

“So now,” Deek interjected, “how are we supposed to get to the other side of that big, humongous hole in the middle of the ground?”

“We jump,” Myles quickly answered.

“Jump?” Naomi confusedly wondered.

“You have any other ideas?” Myles challenged.

“No,” Naomi said.

“But...” Jared began with a little fear in his voice.

“You just saved my life, little brother. If you can do that, I know you have the power to do this. Remember... we walk by faith and not by sight.”

Jared smiled and nodded his head. “Let’s do it.”

Daniel looked over at Brittany and grabbed her hand trying to comfort and assure her. "You ready?" he asked.

Brittany sighed and nodded her head affirming that she was ready to take this literal leap of faith. Brittany and Daniel began to back up a little bit, and then, they both ran at full speed and instantly jumped as high as they could over the hole. Myles, Jared, Naomi, and Deek watched in amazement as Brittany and Daniel landed on the other side.

A few seconds later, Deek sighed and began to prepare herself for the jump; however, Naomi stopped her.

"What are you doing?" Deek asked with a confused expression on her face.

"Let me help you," Naomi said as she held her hand out.

Deek was amazed at the fact that Naomi was offering her assistance. Deek looked at Naomi noticing the sincerity on her face. Deek sighed, and then, she slowly and timidly put her hand in Naomi's. They looked at each other and gave one another a nod. Then, they both backed up, ran full speed, and jumped over the hole landing successfully on the other side.

Myles then held his hand out. "You ready, little brother?"

Jared sighed and placed his hand and his trust in his big brother's hand. "As ready as I'll ever be."

Both boys backed up, and then they ran at full speed and jumped over the hole, but when they both landed, Jared's foot began to slip off the edge of the rock causing him to start to slip. Jared started panicking, but before he gave in to his terror, Myles instantly caught him and pulled him up not allowing his little brother to fall. Jared breathed a sigh a relief, and Myles quickly grabbed him and looked him directly in the eyes with consolation and reinforcement. "I'm always here for you, too," Myles said with a reassuring smile.

Daniel, Brittany, Deek, Naomi, Jared, and Myles took a collective sigh of relief as they realized what they each accomplished together. "Should we continue going?" Brittany asked.

They looked at each other and nonverbally responded with a yes each in their own way. With Myles leading the pack, they continued down the unknown path.

The door of Principal Lawson's door immediately burst open as the head horseman walked in holding a possessed Principal Lawson in his hands. Suddenly, the horseman forcefully pulled the ID badge from Principal Lawson's neck causing Principal Lawson's eye sockets to transform from red back to its original state. Principal Lawson slowly shook his head. "What's going on here?" he asked with confusion.

Then, he saw his chair slowly turning around, and he began to shriek with terror as he saw this large, dark, villainous, creature sitting in his seat. "AHHHHHHHHH!" Principal Lawson screamed. "WHO ARE YOU? WHAT ARE YOU?"

"I am Nefarious," he wickedly snarled. "And I'm your worst nightmare!"

Before Principal Lawson could respond, the horseman robustly hit him in the back of the neck, causing Principal to fall to the ground. Nefarious looked over to see an unconscious Principal Lawson on the ground. Then, he looked at his head horseman and cackled with an evil grin.

Myles, Jared, Naomi, Deek, Brittany, and Daniel continued down the path illuminated by a mysterious light. Then, Brittany looked up and exclaimed, "Look!"

Everyone else looked to see that the light was coming from six crosses on gold chains hanging from a rock formation in the shape of cupping hands. They slowly approached looking at these wonders of illumination in awe. "This is where the light has been coming from," Brittany said.

"What do you think they are?" Naomi wondered.

"I don't know," Myles admitted. "But maybe they'll help us get out of here."

Myles began to walk closer to the glowing crosses, but Jared instantly stopped him. Myles looked back at Jared, who had a concerned look on his face. "Be careful," Jared warned his big brother.

Myles smiled to re-assure his little brother — and himself — that everything would be okay. Myles took a deep breath, and then, he walked closer to the glowing crosses and slowly picked up each cross one by one. After he grabbed the last one, he smiled and excitedly said, "I got them!"

Suddenly, they all started to feel the ground shaking beneath them as they heard a huge rumbling sound. "What's happening?" Naomi wondered.

Myles quickly put the crosses in his pocket, and they each looked to see a huge bolder rolling towards them. "RUN!" Myles shouted.

Daniel, Brittany, Deek, Naomi, Jared, and Myles started to scurry down the only chamber that they could see; they were running and screaming for their lives as the bolder continued to chase after them.

Meanwhile, in Principal Lawson's Office, Nefarious continued to stew in anger and vile as the head horseman rushed in. "Master…"

"What is it?" Nefarious growled.

"The crosses… those children located them."

"Good," Nefarious responded with a sinister smile. "Now, it's time for Phase Two."

As the huge rock continued to roll towards them, getting closer and closer with every second, Daniel, Brittany, Deek, Naomi, Jared, and Myles continued to run as if their lives depended on it. Daniel looked and saw a side entrance that possibly would lead them to their escape. “Look!” he shouted. “Over there!”

Daniel ran towards the side entrance, and the others followed him as the bolder continued to trail them. The brave group of six continued to run until they were inside what appeared to be a hidden cave. Suddenly, the bolder stopped at the entrance trapping them inside. “Oh, thank God that thing stopped chasing us,” Brittany said.

“But we’re trapped inside of this… this cave or whatever this place is,” Deek added.

“What are we going to do now?” Naomi wondered.

Jared started looking around, and then, something caught his peripheral view. There was a small, sparkling glimmer of gold hiding under the dirt on a side of the wall. “What’s that?” Jared asked with a gleam of hope in his eye.

Myles looked and saw it as well. Then, he slowly walked up to it and started wiping off the dirt with his hand. While he was removing the dirt, he began to discover sparkling gold letters written on the wall. “Looks like a hidden message or something,” Myles observed. “Y’all, come and help me uncover the rest.”

Brittany, Jared, Daniel, Deek, and Naomi rushed over and began helping Myles brush the rest of the dirt off the wall to uncover the rest of the hidden, mysterious message. After they finally finished, they each stepped back to see the entire passage shining in gold letters.

"Let no man despise their youth," Daniel began to read.

"For they are examples of love, righteousness, faith, and truth," Naomi continued.

"This prophecy will fulfill, and the Lord is the one who picks," Brittany resumed.

"While the keepers of the crosses," Jared continued to read.

"…are youth of six," Deek slowly read.

"The revelation at the eleventh hour will be the holders of the alignment of power," Myles confusedly finished.

"Youth of six? Alignment of power? I don't get it," Jared admitted.

"What is this supposed to mean?" Deek asked.

"This means that the youth of six…. are you."

Brittany, Jared, Myles, Daniel, Naomi, and Deek each slowly turned around to the sound of that comforting, familiar voice that answered Deek's question, and to their surprise, they saw Michael standing behind them wearing a long, white robe, and suddenly, they each saw a golden sparkle twinkle in his eye.

Meanwhile, back at the Taylor residence, Mr. Taylor was sitting on the couch watching the sports highlights on the television, and Mrs. Taylor entered from the kitchen. "Honey, what time is it?" Mr. Taylor asked his wife.

"It's about 3:30," Mrs. Taylor answered.

"Shouldn't the boys be home by now?"

"Yeah… but maybe they met some new friends, and they're hanging with them."

"Hmmm…. maybe you're right."

Suddenly, the doorbell rang.

"I'll go get it. That may be them now," Mrs. Taylor said.

"But why wouldn't they just use one of their keys?" Mr. Taylor wondered.

"Maybe they forgot them. You know how boys their ages are. You once were one," Mrs. Taylor jokingly said as she walked towards the front door.

"Ha, ha," Mr. Taylor sarcastically responded.

Mrs. Taylor made her way to the door, and she automatically opened without looking through the peephole as she assumed that it was probably their sons. Suddenly, Mrs. Taylor looked, and to her surprise, she saw a big, burly, horse-looking creature standing in front of her.

"AHHHHHHHHHHHHHHHHHHHH!" Mrs. Taylor screamed as the horseman grabbed her and pulled her towards him.

Mr. Taylor heard his wife's screams of terror, and he quickly got off the couch and rushed towards the door. "What's going…"

Suddenly, Mr. Taylor saw the henchman holding his wife.

"AHHHHHHHHHHHHHHHHHHHHHH!" Mr. Taylor screeched as the horseman grabbed him.

Mr. Taylor and Mrs. Taylor began to try and fight the horseman to escape, but his strength proved to be too powerful as he carried them off and away to places unknown.

Myles, Jared, Brittany, Daniel, Naomi, and Deek were standing in their spots seeing what appeared to be Michael standing in front of them. However, they were confused as to what exactly what was happening as they continued to look at him with an expression of bewilderment on their faces. “Michael?” Brittany wondered.

“Yes, it’s me,” Michael confidently affirmed.

“Michael… you’re not really a teacher, are you?” Jared asked.

“No,” Michael answered with a smile. “I am an angel of the Lord, and I have been sent here to help you.”

“Great,” Daniel quickly interjected. “Now, can you please tell us what the heck is going on here?”

“Everyone at the school is possessed,” Naomi frantically told Michael.

“We got scary horse-looking creatures chasing after us,” Deek added.

“We almost died getting here, and now this… prophesy,” Daniel said. “So again, I ask… what the heck is going on here?”

“In due time, my son,” Michael responded in a reassuring manner.

“Well, the time is now!” Daniel demanded.

Brittany gave Daniel a look signaling him to calm down. Then, she turned to Michael, and she asked, “ So... what’s up with them ugly creatures that look like horses?”

"Horsemen," Michael corrected. "And they are Nefarious' henchmen."

"Nefarious? Who is that?" Jared asked.

"Nefarious is ultra-powerful and the most ultimate evil," Michael cautiously answered. "However, if he gets possession of those crosses, then, he will rule over all existence."

"So, our lives are in even more danger now that we have," Myles said as he pulls out the illuminating crosses from his pocket, "these."

"The crosses," Michael said with the smile. Even though he knew the answer, he asked, "So… how did you find them?"

"It was more like they found us," Naomi responded.

"We were just… led to them," Myles added.

"I knew you six were the chosen ones," Michael stated with a bright smile on his face. "The crosses that you are now holding are the keys to a very high power. Whoever has access to these crosses that you speak of possesses that power, which will lead them to becoming the holders of the Armor of God. And since you are now in possession of them, the prophesy has been fulfilled."

"Listen," Deek interjected. "I'm all about things that are… weird, but I'm not sure about any of this. This is just too... freaky for me."

"As the prophesy says, 'This prophesy will fulfill and the Lord picks,'" Michael stated. "The Lord has picked you."

"Why would He pick me?" Deek wondered. "I know nothing about Him, so I'm sure He doesn't know anything about me."

"The Lord knows everything," Michael confidently responded.

"So, Michael, now that we have the crosses, what do we do with them?" Daniel asked.

"Now that you are in possession of the crosses, you must defeat Nefarious and his minions," Michael answered.

"And how are we supposed to do that?" Jared inquired.

"Have faith, young Jared," Michael reassured him.

Jared sighed heavily, but he looked at Michael who smiled at him giving him comfort and confidence. Jared nodded back at Michael responding to his statement.

Michael continued, "As I mentioned before, these crosses possess the ability to activate the Armor of God, which is going to help you defeat Nefarious. Each of you hold a vital piece of this armor."

"How are we supposed to know which piece belongs to us?" Naomi asked.

"May I have the crosses, please?" Michael requested.

Myles looked at Jared, Brittany, Naomi, Daniel, and Deek. Then, they each gave him a nod of approval. Myles slowly walked up to Michael and placed the crosses in Michael's hand.

"Thank you," Michael politely responded with a smile. Then, he walked over to a nearby table made of marble and placed the crosses down on it. Suddenly, the crosses began to illuminate individually in different colors: gold, silver, bronze, blue, purple, and scarlet.

"How do we know which cross belongs to us?" Brittany asked.

"You'll know. Just follow your heart," Michael answered.

Myles slowly walked towards the cross that was illuminating the gold color. After he stood in front of it, a golden lining began to surround him. The others gasped with astonishment. “Oh, my goodness! Look!” Brittany exclaimed.

“He’s shining gold!” Naomi said with excitement.

“Wow!” Jared shouted.

“Well… what are we waiting for?” Daniel wondered. “Let’s do it.”

Daniel, Jared, Naomi, and Brittany began to walk towards the marble as they each followed their hearts standing in front of the crosses that telepathically called out to them. Daniel walked toward the cross that shined bronze as Jared moved towards the cross that had the silver illumination. Meanwhile, Brittany walked in front of the cross with the blue radiation while Naomi stood in front of the purple glowing cross. Suddenly, each color began to illuminate around them: a bronze lining surrounded Daniel, a silver lining surrounded Jared, a blue lining surrounded Brittany, and a purple lining surrounded Naomi. Then, Michael looked to see the that the scarlet cross was the only one left, and he looked over to see Deek standing alone. “Deirdre?” Michael called out.

Deek continued to stand and contemplate what her next move would be. She looked over at others who were standing confidentially in their individual illuminations.

Should I do this? Can I do this? Then, she sighed and slowly walked towards the final cross, and a scarlet lining surrounded her.

"Very good," Michael said. "You have each chosen a weapon that holds a characteristic that each of you strongly possess inside."

Michael walked up to Myles and stood in front of him. Michael picked up the cross and placed the chain around Myles' neck causing the gold lining to disappear. "Myles," Michael began, "you have chosen the Gold cross, which holds the Sword of the Spirit. Remember the Word of God is sharper than the sharpest two-edged sword, cutting between soul and spirit, between joint and marrow."

Then, Michael moved to Daniel, picked up the bronze cross, and placed the chain around Daniel's neck resulting in the bronze lining to disappear. "Daniel, you have chosen the Bronze cross, which holds the Breastplate of Righteousness. Never forget that God is working in you. Let His righteousness be your guide."

Michael continued towards Jared, picked up the silver cross, and placed the chain around Jared's neck, which subsequently made the silver lining disappear. "Young Jared… you have chosen the Silver cross, which holds the Shield of Faith. Faith is the substance of things hoped for and the evidence of things not seen. Continue to have faith, Jared. Have faith."

Jared smiled hopefully as Michael walked over to Brittany, and he picked up the blue cross and placed the chain around her neck. "Brittany, you have chosen the Blue cross, which holds the Foot Shod of The Gospel of Peace. And the peace of God, which passes all understanding, will keep your heart and mind through Christ Jesus."

Michael then moved to Naomi, picked up the purple cross, and placed the chain around her neck, which caused the purple lining to disappear from around her. "Naomi, you have chosen the Purple cross which holds the Belt of Truth."

"Belt of Truth? Me?" Naomi questioned with a scoff. "All I do is lie."

"And why is that?" Michael challenged.

"I… I…"

"The truth shall set you free, Naomi. Remember, Jesus is the way, the ***truth***, and the life," Michael said.

Naomi nodded her head and smiled as Michael walked over to Deek and stood in front of her. He picked up the scarlet cross and placed the chain around her neck, and the scarlet lining disappeared from her around her. "And last but certainly not least, there is Deirdre. You have chosen the Scarlet cross, which holds the Helmet of Salvation."

"Salvation? Me?" Deek wondered.

"Yes, you," Michael continued. "Deirdre, don't let your circumstances prohibit you from receiving this free gift that is available to you."

"Free gift?" Deek contested. "Nothing in life is free."

"Salvation is," Michael gracefully responded.

"Listen, Deek, none of us know why we're here," Naomi interjected. "But for some reason, we are."

"We are the chosen ones. The fate of the world lies in our hands," Brittany added.

"We can't do this without you," Jared said to her trying to ease and comfort her mind.

Deek began to contemplate what they were saying to her. Then, she sighed and said to Michael, "Fine."

Michael resumed, "Guard your mind, Deek. Don't let anyone despise who you are. Remember that you are loved. We love you, but most importantly, Jesus loves you."

Deek slightly smiled as she looked at everyone else who was looking at her beaming with glee.

"Together, you all possess the entire Armor of God and are now the holders of the alignment of power!" Michael exclaimed.

"How do we possess this… power?" Myles wondered.

"You begin with putting your arms together as an X, and then, you bring your hands around in a cupping formation," Michael instructed.

"Why a cupping formation?" Daniel asked.

"When Jesus washed the feet of His disciples, he used his very own hands," Michael informed. "The cupping formation is to remind you that even though you have this ultimate power, you are to use this power to serve others and to serve the world. Now, once you have done the correct hand formation, call out in faith: IT... IS… WRITTEN. After that, you shall receive the power that each of you possess through your individual armors. And collectively, you shall be known as the… TITAN WARRIORS!"

Daniel, Myles, Brittany, Jared, and Naomi looked at each other with excitement and amazement; however, Deek had an unsure and uncomfortable expression on her face. She still was not sure if she was making the right decision or if she could trust anything that was happening… or anyone.

Brittany looked behind Daniel and noticed something blinking on his back. “Daniel, hold still.”

Daniel had a confused look on his face as Brittany reached behind him and removed the strange looking device from the back of this shirt. “What is this?” she wondered.

“It looks like some sort of tracking device,” Naomi responded.

“It probably was placed on you when that horseman grabbed you,” Myles assumed.

“Which means by now, Nefarious is fully aware that you all are in possession of the crosses, and you need to know that he is willing to do whatever it takes to get them… even if that means destroying you,” Michael said.

“And we’re willing to do anything it takes to keep them from him… even if that means killing him,” Myles confidentially responded.

“And how do we do that?” Naomi asked. “How do we kill Nefarious exactly?”

"With a sword… in the heart," Michael informed. "That is how you will defeat Nefarious."

"Then, I guess it's up to me," Myles responded.

"It's up to all of us," Daniel corrected. "Teamwork, remember?"

"That's correct," Michael said. "It's going to take all of you to defeat Nefarious. Remember, be strong and courageous. God has not given you a Spirit of fear, but of power, love, and a sound mind."

After Michael finished his encouraging speech, one of the walls of the hidden cave opened, revealing the sunlight shining from the outside. Deek immediately and hurriedly stormed out of the cave. With worried looks on their faces, everyone else looked at Michael, but Michael smiled giving them his blessing to follow behind her. Jared, Myles, Daniel, Brittany, and Naomi walked out of the cave. As they were exiting, a golden spark twinkled in Michael's eyes. "Godspeed," he said as he watched the new, young heroes continue on the journey that would change their lives and the fate of the world forever.

CHAPTER NINE

Deek stormed out of the cave and continued walking down the clay dirt road not really paying attention to her new surroundings of the desert landscape with red clay mountain-type structures. Her only goal was to get back to some sense of normalcy… or whatever that meant to her. Even though she did not know exactly where she was going, Deek continued down the unknown path even though she could hear a familiar voice calling out to her.

"Deek, wait!"

Deek sighed, but then, she decided to ignore Jared's voice as she continued walking as a few small rocks began to fall from the structures. Suddenly, dark clouds started to form in the sky as the thunder rolled quietly. However, Jared was able to catch up with Deek, and he grabbed her and exclaimed making sure he had her attention, "Deek!"

Deek instantly snatched away from Jared and shouted, "What?"

"What are you doing?" Jared asked.

"I'm doing what I should've done in the first place!" Deek responded. "Walked away from all of this… and all of you."

"Why?" Jared wondered.

"I can't do this, Jared!" Deek honestly said with fear and timidity in her voice. "I can't be some multi-colored, spandex-wearing superhero trying to save the world from some horsemen or some big, bad supernatural monster. I can't fight evil! Look at me!"

"I am! And you can!" Jared exclaimed with encouragement. "Besides, we need you! And you need us!"

"What's the point?"

"After all we've been through today…. you still don't trust us?"

"What's the point to trust in people? Huh?" Deek challenged. "All they are going to do is disappoint you, abandon you… forget about you."

Jared lightly touched Deek's shoulder with comfort. "Trust in Jesus," he said with reassurance. "He'll never let you down."

However, Deek immediately moved Jared's hand, and she cried out with frustration, "Jesus… Jesus… I swear if I hear that name one more time, I'ma scream!"

Suddenly, a flying horseman with big black wigs and large claws swooped down and picked Deek up by her shoulders carrying her into the air.

"AHHHHHHHHHHHHHHHHHHHHHHHH!" Deek screeched with fear.

"Deek!" Jared yelled as Myles, Brittany, Naomi, and Daniel finally caught up to him.

"What happened?" Myles wondered.

"They stole Deek!" Jared frantically shouted. "They got Deek!"

Myles, Brittany, Naomi, and Daniel looked up to see the flying horseman carrying Deek with his claws in the partially darkened sky. "Oh no!" Brittany worriedly exclaimed.

"Let me go!" Deek demanded.

"Not until you give me that cross," the flying horseman said.

"Buzz off, you horse-faced, bird-legged freak!" Deek insulted. "Now let me go!"

"Okay. You asked for it."

Suddenly, the flying horseman released Deek from his claws, and Deek started falling from the air.

"AHHHHHHHHHHHHHHHHHHHHHHHH!" Deek screamed.

As she was falling, Deek began to cry with terror. *This is it. This is how my life ends. Jesus... please save me.*

Deek then closed her eyes as she began to accept the possibility that her life was about to come to an end. However, just before Deek hits the ground, Jared ran under her and caught her in his arms. "Gotcha!"

Deek opened her eyes realizing that she was safe in Jared's arms. She stammered, "How did you… why did you…"

"I told you… just trust me," Jared responded with a smile.

Deek smiled back at him as Jared carefully placed her down on her feet. Myles, Daniel, Brittany, and Naomi ran up to them.

"Deek, you alright?" Myles asked.

"Yeah, I'm good," Deek said. "Thanks to Jared."

"Dang, little brother, I didn't know you were so strong," Myles admitted.

"Neither did I, but I just reminded myself that I can do all things through Christ who strengthens me," Jared responded.

Myles patted Jared on the back with pride. However, there was not enough time to celebrate as they looked up to see a big group of horsemen gathering towards them. Suddenly, the head horseman galloped in on his steed as he steered it towards the young heroes positioning themselves in front of the big group of evil henchmen. Deek, Jared, Myles, Daniel, Brittany, and Naomi stood close together as the horsemen began to angrily snarl and growl at them. "Give up those crosses!" the head horseman demanded.

"Not on your life!" Deek shouted.

"If you don't give them to us, we will just have to TAKE THEM!" the head horseman threatened.

"Then, you're gonna have to take them, horse-face!" Brittany yelled.

"Then, we'll fight," the head horseman retorted. "TO THE DEATH!"

"If it's a fight you want, it's a fight you're gonna get!" Daniel challenged.

“Hey,” Myles said to his comrades, “I think it’s time we try these new powers out.”

Daniel, Brittany, Jared, Deek, and Naomi nodded in agreement as they all stood in their battle-ready positions. Then, they each remembered Michael’s instructions to call upon their new abilities as they put their arms together forming an X, and then, they brought their hands together in a cupping position. Immediately, they all shouted, “IT… IS… WRITTEN!”

Suddenly, each of their crosses lit up in their individual colors, and a large light began to fill the atmosphere.

“BELT OF TRUTH!” Naomi called out. Then, her battle armor, which was a black shinobi shozoku base, began to cover her body, and then, a purple belt with a purple cross buckle began to wrap around her waist as she transformed into the PURPLE TITAN WARRIOR.

“BREASTPLATE OF RIGHTEOUSNESS!” Daniel called out. Then, his battle armor, which was also the black shinobi shozoku base, began to cover his body, and then, a bronze breastplate with a cross on the front began to cover his chest as he transformed into the BRONZE TITAN WARRIOR.

"FOOT SHOD OF THE GOSPEL OF PEACE!" Brittany called out as her battle armor including the black shinobi shozoku base began to cover body, and then, blue footwear with a cross on each side began to appear on her feet as she transformed into the BLUE TITAN WARRIOR.

"SHIELD OF FAITH!" Jared excitedly shouted as his battle armor including the black shinobi shozoku base began to cover his body, and then, he held his hand out, and a silver shield with a cross on the front appeared as he transformed into the SILVER TITAN WARRIOR.

"HELMET OF SALVATION!" Deek called out as her battle armor, which included the black shinobi shozoku base, started covering her body, and a scarlet helmet with a cross on top of it appeared on her head as she transformed into the SCARLET TITAN WARRIOR.

"SWORD OF THE SPIRIT!" Myles exclaimed as his battle armor, which included the black shinobi shozoku base, began to cover his body, and he held his hand out, and a gold sword appeared as he transformed into the GOLD TITAN WARRIOR.

After the light faded away, Daniel, Brittany, Deek, Naomi, Jared, and Myles boldly stood together in unity, and they shouted out courageously, "TITAN WARRIORS!"

Immediately, the head horseman cackled, "That's cute." Then, he yelled ferociously, "ATTACK!!!!!!"

The horsemen instantly began to charge towards the Titan Warriors while the young heroes each prepared to attack and fight their enemies.

Several horsemen ran towards Daniel, but Daniel was not afraid as he met them halfway. Daniel punched one of the horsemen in the face, and he kicked another horseman in the chest causing them both to fall to the ground. Suddenly, two other horsemen grabbed Daniel by the arms holding him with all their might causing him to struggle to get away from them. However, unbeknownst to them, Myles snuck up behind one of the horsemen and sliced him in the back with his sword causing him to fall to the ground. Then, Daniel roundhouse kicked the other horseman causing him to fall to the ground.

"You alright?" Myles asked.

"Yeah," Daniel answered.

However, while they were talking, a horseman began to run up behind Myles with his sword about to attack him from behind. Daniel saw him and warned, "Watch out!"

Myles turned around to see the horseman coming towards him, but Daniel quickly stood in front of Myles, and just as the horseman was about to strike, Daniel's breastplate lit up, and a force field was placed around Myles and Daniel prohibiting the horseman from the hitting them. However, the energy exuded from the force field hit the horseman causing him to fall to the ground.

"What was that?" Myles wondered with curiosity.

"Force field powers, I guess," Daniel responded.

Meanwhile, a few horsemen pulled out their bow and arrows and shot their arrows towards Jared. Jared quickly covered himself with his shield, and the arrows bounced off it. After their failed attempt to hit him, the horsemen began charging towards Jared. When they approached him, Jared kicked one of the horsemen in the kneecap knocking him to the ground. Then, Jared kicked another horseman in the chest causing him to collapse to the ground as well. Two more horsemen stormed towards Jared, but he immediately knocked them down using his shield. Then, Jared looked over to see Naomi fighting a horseman; however, another horseman began to sneak up behind her without her knowledge. Jared then retracted his arm back with his shield in his hand, and with all this strength, Jared slung the Shield of Faith at the horseman. After a few seconds of gliding through the air, the shield hit the horseman in the back of the head knocking him completely out.

Naomi continued to fight the horseman that was directly attacking her. After a few more seconds of scuffling, Naomi forcefully punched the horseman in the face causing him to fall on the ground. However, to her surprise, Naomi was knocked down to the ground herself after being unexpectedly kicked by another horseman. That horseman then stood over her in an intimidating manner growling and snarling, and Naomi looked up at him with fear. Suddenly, the horseman pulled out his sword and held it towards her getting ready to stab her. Naomi immediately began to nestle with trepidation, and just as the sword was about to pierce her flesh, Naomi grabbed the Belt of Truth tightly and suddenly disappeared. The horseman started looking around with a stunned and confused look on his dark and terrifying face. As the horseman was searching for his vanishing victim, he felt someone tapping him on the shoulder. The horseman turned around, and to his disbelief, he saw Naomi standing behind. Suddenly, she punched him in the face, and it knocked him down to the ground. "Don't you ever kick me like that again, you freak!" Naomi demanded.

Jared rushed towards her. "How did you disappear like that?" he wondered as he grabbed the Shield of Faith.

"I dunno," Naomi admitted. "I just clutched tight to my belt and closed my eyes, and the next thing I know, I was standing behind the horseman who was trying to kill me."

"Man, I love these new powers!" Jared excitedly exclaimed.

Suddenly, several horsemen started rushing towards Naomi and Jared, and they stood in their battle stances ready to take them on.

In the meantime, one horseman started running towards Brittany ready to attack her, but Brittany quickly dodged out of his way. Two more horsemen began to charge towards her with their swords ready to slice her in half. "AHHHHHHHHHHHHHHHHHHHHHHHHHH!" Brittany screamed with terror.

As the horsemen were vastly approaching her, the Foot Shod of the Gospel of Peace began to glow on her feet. Suddenly, Brittany began to run, but this time, she was running in warp-speed. Milliseconds later, she was on the other side of the horsemen. "What in the world?" she said with amazement.

But she did not have time to figure out what was happening as the horsemen began to run after her. Immediately, her feet started glowing again, and Brittany resumed running at escape velocity quickly exceeding the horsemen.

Deek watched with wonder as the horsemen continued to chase after Brittany, but they proved to be able to keep up with her. She looked in one area to see Jared and Naomi fighting horsemen and Daniel and Myles fighting more henchmen in another area. Suddenly, she heard growling nearby, and she turned her head and saw several horsemen rushing towards her on their horses. Deek had a fearful expression on her face. In frustration, Deek clutched the Helmet of Salvation with her hands and yelled. Suddenly, the cross from the helmet shot out lasers hitting the horsemen and causing them to fall of their horses. They immediately hit the ground, and the horses ran away in terror. "Wow," Deek said in shock.

While Daniel was fighting the horsemen, Myles looked over to see Brittany running away from the ones chasing her. Wanting to come to her rescue, Myles quickly jumped high in the air, and he landed right in front of the horsemen stopping them from trying to attack Brittany. "How about you mess with someone your own size?" Myles threatened trying to be intimidating.

However, the horsemen started attacking Myles. Myles kicked one horseman, and he successfully knocked him to the ground. However, another horseman grabbed Myles from behind causing him to drop the Sword of the Spirit. Then, the other horseman began punching Myles in the chest. Myles cried out in pain as each punch landed harder than the last one.

Brittany stopped running to see Myles being beaten by the horsemen that were once chasing after her. She saw that her teammate was in trouble. Then, she quickly ran back towards them at warp speed. Suddenly, she started running around the horsemen and Myles creating a huge whirlwind of dirt. The horsemen began to cough as they were being blinded by the earth. Brittany then stopped running around them. After the dirt cyclone died down, the horsemen looked around to see that Brittany and Myles were no longer among them.

"YAHHHHHHHHHHHHHHH!"

The horsemen looked up to see Brittany and Myles coming down towards them from up in the air. Then, they both kicked the horsemen in their faces causing them to fall immediately to the ground.

"Thanks for the save," Myles said to Brittany,

"Let's just say… I owed you one," Brittany responded.

However, as Brittany was talking, the head horseman rode up behind her with his sword, and he began to swing it preparing to chop off Brittany's head. "Look out!" Myles cried out as he pushed Brittany out of the way, grabbed the Sword of the Spirit, and hit the horseman's sword.

As both swords collided, the head horseman growled in Myles' face. "Give it up, kid!" he snarled.

"Never!" Myles shouted.

The head horseman and Myles continued fighting with their swords; however, Myles appeared to be struggling a little bit. Suddenly, the horse held his hooves up and kicked Myles in the chest knocking him to the ground and knocking the wind out of Myles.

"Myles!" Brittany yelled as she ran and kneeled to him. "Are you alright?"

"Yeah," Myles said painfully coughing. "I'm good."

Daniel, Deek, Jared, and Naomi quickly ran to Brittany and Myles.

"Myles!" Jared exclaimed with a worried look on his face wondering if his brother was alright. Then, his expression changed to anger as he turned towards the head horseman. "Alright, now! You done did it now!"

"Give it up!" the head horseman snarled. "You're nothing but pathetic children! You will NEVER defeat Nefarious! Give up those crosses NOW!"

"I'm not going to let anyone despise or talk down to us because we're young," Jared boldly declared. "And I refuse to let some ugly horse creature like you do it to us!"

While Jared made his declaration, Brittany helped Myles stand up, and they both rejoined the other Titan Warriors. "It's time to kick some horseman butt… Titan Warriors style!" Daniel brazenly announced.

"Let's get him, Warriors!" Myles shouted.

The Titan Warriors began to run towards the head horseman. Myles began attacking him with the Sword of the Spirit, but the horseman fought back at full strength with his sword. Daniel jumped in the air trying to attack him from above, but before Daniel could kick him, the head horseman hit him in the chest knocking him down to the ground. Naomi and Brittany both flipped towards the horseman and tried kicking him from both sides, but they missed. Then, the horseman instantly knocked them down. The horseman began to ride towards Deek, and just as he was about to strike her with his sword, Jared quickly stood in front of Deek blocking it with the Shield of Faith. Jared pushed the horseman away causing him and his horse to fall back a little.

"You alright?" Jared asked Deek.

"Yeah," Deek responded. "Now, it's my turn."

Deek puts her head on her helmet and yells out a victorious battle cry, "AHHHHHHHHHHHHHHHHHH!"

Suddenly, the cross on the Helmet of Salvation shot out lasers blasting the head horseman. Deek continued shooting the lasers, and all the blasts knocked the horseman off his horse. As the head horseman fell to the ground, his trusted steed frantically ran away. The horseman looked as if he was trying to get up, but Deek resumed blasting more lasers at him hitting the horseman. After a few more hits, the head horseman stopped moving. Myles, Brittany, Naomi, and Daniel got up off the ground and rejoined Jared and Deek as they surrounded the motionless head horseman.

"Now," Myles wondered. "Where is Nefarious?"

"I'M RIGHT HERE!" they heard a vile voice coming from above.

The Titan Warriors looked up towards the highest mountain, and they saw Nefarious standing at the ledge. "Give me those crosses, now!" he revoltingly demanded.

"You want them?" Myles challenged. "Come and get them!"

"I bet you'll change your tune after you see this!" Nefarious wickedly responded.

Then, he stepped to the side revealing a cage that contained Mr. and Mrs. Taylor, Principal Lawson, Daniel's parents, and Brittany's parents blindfolded, gagged, and tied together.

"Oh no!" Myles shouted.

"He has our parents!" Naomi screamed.

"What are you doing with our parents?" Daniel angrily yelled.

"It's simple," Nefarious nonchalantly responded. "You give me the crosses, and I'll spare the lives of your parentals."

"And if we don't?" Myles contested.

"THEY'RE AS GOOD AS DEAD!" Nefarious snarled.

"Myles, what do we do?" Brittany asked in a terrified voice.

"Time is waiting... AND I'M NOT VERY PATIENT!" Nefarious evilly roared as he slowly began to push the cage off the ledge sinisterly laughing as he tried to taunt the young heroes into making a decision.

The parents could barely scream for their lives, but they continued to yell with all their might. The Titan Warriors were frightened, and they had no idea what to do. If they did not give Nefarious the crosses, they would lose their parents forever. If they surrendered the crosses, Nefarious would be in possession of the Armor of God and the fate of the world would be eternally doomed.

However, the cage continued to move closer and closer over the ledge. Myles knew what he unfortunately had to do. "STOP!" he yelled.

Nefarious stopped pushing the cage, and the other warriors looked at Myles waiting with bated breath on the next words that would come out of his mouth.

"We'll give you the crosses!" Myles regrettably and sadly continued.

Nefarious cackled. "That's what I thought."

"Alright guys... you know what we gotta do next," Myles woefully said to the others.

"How do we power down?" Jared wondered.

"I have an idea," Myles responded. Then, he yelled, "IT... IS... FINISHED!"

Suddenly, Myles' battle armor and the Sword of the Spirit dissolved, and Myles was back in his regular clothes. He sadly looked at the others and nodded at them to follow suit. "IT... IS... FINISHED!" they unhappily cried out as each of their battle armors and their individual pieces of the Armor of God dissolved.

Myles watched with gloom as his teammates were now back in their regular clothes as well. Then, Myles looked up to Nefarious, and his countenance changed from sadness to anger. "Now... release our parents," he said.

"Throw the crosses to me now!" Nefarious ordered.

"You release our parents first!" Myles yelled back.

"I GIVE THE ORDERS AROUND HERE YOU PUBESCENT, PUTRENT PIECE OF HUMAN FLESH!" Nefarious screamed with vile and disgust. "NOW, THROW

ME THE CROSSES OR YOUR PARENTS WILL BE DESTROYED!"

Myles looked at Daniel, Brittany, Deek, Naomi, and Jared, and immediately, each of them took the chains off their necks and gave them to Myles. Then, Myles took the chain off his neck. He looked at the crosses as they each continued to illuminate. Then, he sadly sighed, and with all the strength that he had, he threw them up and towards Nefarious. The teenagers could see each of the crosses shining brightly in their individual colors in the sky. But suddenly, Nefarious clasped them with his big, evil grip. However, after he had them in his hand, he looked down at the young heroes, and then, he swiftly pushed the cage with their parents trapped inside off the mountain. "Oops," he sarcastically chortled.

"AHHHHHHHHHHHHHHHHHHHHHHHHHHH!" the parents yelled even though the screams were muffled through the gag.

"NOOOOOOOOOOOOOOOOOOOOOOOOOOO!" the young heroes cried out as they watched their parents fall to their doom.

Suddenly, Michael appeared with his wide, white wings spread out and his sword by his side. He swooped in and caught the cage by its chain. The adolescents watched their guardian angel with relief on their faces as Michael placed the cage down on the ground. As Michael lightly landed on his feet on the other side at the foot of the mountain and lowered his wings, Myles, Jared, Daniel, Brittany, Naomi, and Deek quickly ran up to him with excitement and jubilation. "Michael!" Deek shouted.

"Thank you so much for saving our parents!" Naomi exclaimed.

"Now, let's rescue them," Jared said earnestly ready to free his parents.

"No. It's safer to leave them where they are," Michael instructed.

"Michael," Myles regrettably began, "I'm sorry."

"Sorry for what?" Michael asked even though he already knew the answer.

"I'm sorry that we gave Nefarious the crosses," Myles continued. "But we had our parents, and..."

"I understand," Michael assuredly responded. "You made a hard, but wise decision. There's no need to fret, my friends. Everything will be okay. I promise."

The young heroes smiled at their heavenly mentor, and then, Michael looked up towards Nefarious.

"NEFARIOUS, GIVE UP THOSE CROSSES!" Michael demanded with a booming voice.

"YOU'RE TOO LATE, MICHAEL! THE POWER IS ALL MINE!" Nefarious cackled.

Suddenly, Nefarious crushed the crosses with little to no effort, and suddenly, all the light and power that was in the crosses transferred to Nefarious. The young heroes watched with horrified looks on their faces as Nefarious' body began to illuminate. Suddenly, Nefarious started to grow until he was ten times his normal size. The helmet on his head fell off, and his face transformed into this dragon-like monster. Suddenly, he sprouted out five more heads from his neck. The teenagers looked at the newly transformed Nefarious with terrified expressions on their faces as he growled in terror and towered over the entire city.

"THIS CITY IS MINE!" Nefarious loudly gloated. "THE WHOLE ENTIRE UNIVERSE IS MINE!"

Nefarious began stomping towards the city causing the ground to tremble.

"How are we going to defeat Nefarious especially now that he's like this?" Brittany asked with frightened look on her face.

"Remember," Michael calmly responded, "the battle is not ours. It's the Lord's."

Suddenly, Michael's wings expanded out widely, and Michael flew towards Nefarious strongly and mightily carrying his sword in his hand. Then, he flew right in front of Nefarious' main face. "Stop right there!"

"Who are you to stop me?" Nefarious laughed.

"I am an angel of the Lord!" Michael said in a resounding tone. "And the Lord is ALWAYS victorious!"

"Not today He's not!" Nefarious maliciously retorted.

Immediately, one of Nefarious' other heads reached towards Michael trying to gobble him up, but Michael swiftly dodged it. However, another head tried to devour him as well, but this time, it barely missed him. Michael took his sword and swiped it at Nefarious trying to strike him. Michael made an aim for Nefarious' dark heart with the sword, but Nefarious was guarding it heavily with his several heads.

Meanwhile, Myles, Jared, Daniel, Brittany, Naomi, and Deek watched from below at the battle between Michael and Nefarious. "Y'all, we have to help Michael!" Brittany worriedly exclaimed.

"But how?" Deek asked. "We don't have any powers!"

"Yes, we do," Myles retorted.

"Uhhhh... did you miss the whole situation with Nefarious taking our crosses and stealing the powers to grow into that ugly, hideous, six-headed monster?" Daniel sarcastically wondered.

"No, I didn't," Myles answered. "The reason why we are the chosen ones is because we had the power within us the entire time. All we have to do is have faith and believe in ourselves, and I know that without a shadow of a doubt that we can defeat Nefarious."

Myles confidently put out his hand. "Sword of the Spirit!"

Jared smiled and put his hand on top of his big brother's. "Shield of Faith!"

"Belt of Truth!" Naomi bolted out putting her hand on top of Jared's.

"Foot Shod of the Gospel of Peace!" Brittany shouted following suit.

"Breastplate of Righteousness!" Daniel exclaimed put his hand on hers.

Lastly, Deek put her hand on Daniel's and yelled, "Helmet of Salvation!"

Suddenly, gold, silver, bronze, blue, purple, and scarlet colors began to shine over their hands. "Let's do it!" Myles shouted.

Then, they pulled their hands apart ready to take on whatever came their way. "So, what's the game plan?" Daniel asked.

"Nefarious is defeated once Michael can stab him in the heart with the sword," Myles reminded them.

"But how can he? Nefarious has six heads!" Jared exclaimed. "I mean, I know that two heads are better than one, but goodness gracious!"

Suddenly, an idea came to Myles. "That's it! We need to distract Nefarious!"

"But how?" Naomi wondered.

"Follow my lead," Myles instructed.

Myles quickly ran over towards Nefarious, and the others followed behind him. While Michael continued his battle with Nefarious, the young heroes began to surround Nefarious.

"Give it up, Angel Boy!" Nefarious taunted. "You'll never win! The kids failed, and now, you're going to lose!"

"Hey, Dragon Breath!" Myles shouted.

Nefarious looked down to see Myles standing behind him.

"You want a piece of me?" Myles continued.

Immediately, one of Nefarious' heads moved towards Myles to attack him, but Myles dodged it.

"Hey! If you want some, come and get some!" Daniel yelled.

Then, another head stretched towards Daniel trying to consume him, but Daniel swiftly moved out of the way avoiding it.

"Nah, nah, nah, boo-boo. You can't get me!" Naomi taunted from another side.

A third head extended towards her, but it missed her.

"Hey, don't leave me out of all the fun!" Brittany joked as the fourth head extended out to her trying to grab her.

"This is for almost killing my parents!" Jared shouted, and he kicked Nefarious in the leg.

"You think that hurt?" Nefarious jeered. "Now, it's time for some real hurt! You're mine, you little punk!"

Suddenly, a fifth head moved towards Jared to attack him, but Jared was able to dodge it.

"Hey, ugly!" Deek yelled.

Nefarious looked at Deek. "Well, isn't that the pot calling the kettle black?" he mocked.

"Well, I'm not the one with six heads, you freak!" Deek derisively shouted.

The final head stretched out trying to grab Deek, but it missed. Now, all the heads were distracted by the young heroes. "For the Lord our God is like a consuming fire," Michael declared. "Reign down your mighty power, O Mighty God, our Abba Father! Reign down on us!"

Suddenly, Michael's sword lit up with flames. As the fire began to consume his almighty weapon, Michael swiftly flew towards Nefarious. However, just as Brittany continued to taunt Nefarious' other head, not seeing the huge rock that fell beside her, she tripped over it falling hard on the ground.

"Now, I gotcha!" Nefarious sneered.

"AHHHHHHHHHHHHHHHHHHHH!" Brittany screamed in terror.

Just as Nefarious' sinister head was about to devour Brittany, Michael reached Nefarious' chest and stabbed him in the heart with his flaming sword. Immediately, Nefarious stopped moving. Michael quickly pulled the sword out, and suddenly, black, rancid, vile liquid began to pour out of Nefarious' chest. The teenagers watched with disgusted looks on their faces as Nefarious' other subsequent heads swiveled up into non-existence. Then, Nefarious began to shrink back down to his original size. They all watched as Nefarious fell to the ground lying down on his back with defeat. As the dark, foul liquid continued to leak from his dark hard exiting his body, Nefarious slowly began to disappear.

While Michael landed softly on the ground retracting his wings, Myles ran over to Brittany and helped her off the ground. Myles and Brittany looked each other in the eyes making a connection. While their hands were intertwined and their eyes were locked into each other, Daniel quickly ran over to Brittany, and then, she moved her hand away from Myles.

"Babe, you alright?" Daniel asked.

Brittany had to snap back to reality realizing that it was her boyfriend who was talking to her. "Yeah, yeah. I'm good."

After that brief yet subtly awkward exchange, Brittany, Daniel, and Myles rejoined Jared, Naomi, and Deek, and then, all six of them ran over to Michael, who was standing over Nefarious' disappearing being. "It's... not... over," Nefarious threatened in between breaths. "I will.... be back!"

After his final gasp, Nefarious completely vanished. There was nothing left but the disgusting black liquid from his rancid heart on the ground. Meanwhile, on the battleground, all the defeated horsemen who were lying on the ground also disappeared into the thin air.

Back at Rowlands High School, all the students, teachers, and other faculty members were still under the mind-control as they continued to destroy the hallways. Suddenly, the ID badges began to fall off their necks, and all their eye sockets turned from red back to their natural eye colors. After a few seconds of disorientation, they all began to look around at their disastrous surroundings trying to figure out what was going on as they also looked at each other with confusion and bewilderment.

Meanwhile, back at the war zone, Michael placed his sword inside its holder on his hip. He looked at the young warriors with pride beaming from his face. "Congratulations! Nefarious has been defeated. You all helped saved your city... and ultimately, you saved the entire world."

"But what about everyone else at the school?" Naomi asked.

"Now that Nefarious has been vanquished, all of your classmates and your teachers have been freed from his mind control," Michael answered.

"What about the horsemen?" Brittany wondered.

"They're gone as well."

"But what about the crosses?" Myles inquired.

Michael sighed. "As you saw, the crosses were sadly destroyed," he honestly responded. "But as you have also discovered, the power is still in each and every one of you. It always has been, and it always will be."

"And... what about you?" Deek questioned.

Michael sighed again. He knew that the response that he was about to give them would not be a favorable one especially for Deek. "I must return back to Heaven... and receive my next assignment."

Deek sadly moved closer to Michael and took his hand in hers. "Will we ever see you again?" she unhappily asked trying not to shed a tear.

Brittany, Jared, Myles, Daniel, and Naomi also looked at Michael with sorrow in their eyes. Michael could see the sadness on his young protégé's faces, but he knew that he had to comfort them in some way before his departure. "Fear not," he said. "For the Lord Your God will always be with you. He will never leave you nor forsake you. He will always be with you even until the end of the world. And with that promise, always remember that you have His love within you and the love of one another surrounding you. Never forget that."

After his words of affirmation, Michael released Deek's hand. Suddenly, he spread his wings, and he began to fly away. The teens looked up and yelled, "Goodbye, Michael!"

"Goodbye, my young warriors!" Michael shouted gleefully. "And thank you... for everything!"

They continued to watch as Michael ascended into the sky and after a few more seconds, he disappeared into the clouds. Then, they looked at each other and sighed sadly as they finally came to the realization that their heavenly mentor was gone not knowing when or if he would ever return.

After a few more moments of disappointment and sadness, Daniel snapped back to reality. “Our parents!” he shouted as he ran back towards the battlegrounds where the cage where their parents were locked up was located.

Myles, Jared, Brittany, Naomi, and Deek swiftly followed behind Daniel, and they approached the cage where their parents were still tied up, blindfolded, and gagged. They all began to frantically look for something to pick the lock. Then, Myles looked and saw a big rock nearby, and he picked up and banged the lock with the rock until it broke and fell off. Myles immediately opened the gate, and he pulled Mr. and Mrs. Taylor out of the cage. Jared assisted his big brother, and they united, ungagged, and removed the blindfolds off Mr. and Mrs. Taylor. Mr. and Mrs. Taylor saw their sons, and they quickly kissed them and hugged them tightly.

The other adolescents, except Deek, followed suit as Naomi pulled out Principal Lawson and Brittany and Daniel pulled out their parents, and they freed them from their captivity. While the parents were loving on their children and rejoicing in their safety, Deek watched with sadness in her eyes. A tear began to fall as she turned around and slowly walked away. However, Jared looked and watched Deek sorrowfully isolate herself. "Deek, wait!" he called out.

Deek stopped and turned around to see Jared running towards her, and he grabbed her and hugged her. Deek was confused yet overwhelmed with gladness. *What is going on here? What is happening? Whatever this is... I'm happy it's finally happening to me.*

Then, she slowly put her arms around Jared, and she hugged him back. After their sweet, tender moment, Jared grabbed Deek's hand and brought her back over to everyone else. Then, they all formed a big circle and gave each other a big group hug. The love, happiness, thankfulness, and gratitude could be felt all over the entire atmosphere. After they finished their celebratory embrace, Jared looked around and wondered, "Now, how are we supposed to get back home exactly?"

"Looks like we're going to be using Ike and Mike," Mr. Taylor answered.

Deek, Jared, Myles, Daniel, Naomi, and Brittany looked at each other with confused expressions on their faces. "Huh?"

All the parents laughed together at the cluelessness of their offspring as they understood what Mr. Taylor meant by his statement. So, after a little explanation, Deek, Jared, Myles, Mr. and Mrs. Taylor, Naomi, Principal Lawson, Daniel, Brittany, and their parents began their voyage back towards home as the sun started to set and the peace that passes all understanding began to rest over Garden City.

CHAPTER TEN

SIZZZZZZZLLLLLLLEEEEEE!

The sound of the beginnings of a cookout could be heard across the neighborhood as Mr. Taylor was broiling fresh ground turkey burger patties and turkey dogs on the grill. Mrs. Taylor walked outside carrying paper plates and cups and placed them on the table.

It had been a few days since Nefarious' failed attempt to find the crosses and take over the world, and everything and everyone appeared to be trying to get back to some sense of normalcy as if nothing happened. Naomi and Jared were sitting on the steps talking and laughing. Meanwhile, in the driveway, Myles was shooting hoops with his basketball. Myles then positioned himself at the three-point mark and threw the ball in the air.

SWOOSH!

Nothing but net as the ball went through the hoop and landed on the ground. Myles proudly walked over and picked up the ball, and after he did, he looked up to see Brittany walking towards him. “Hi,” he greeted.

“Hey,” she politely said.

Suddenly, there was awkward silence between them.

After a few seconds, they both unintentional blurted out at the same time, “Listen!”

“You first,” Myles insisted.

“I just want to say… thank you.”

“Thank you?” Myles wondered. “For what?”

“For… everything,” Brittany sweetly responded. “You’re a great leader… a great friend… just an all-around great guy.”

Myles began to blush a little bit… even if it could not be seen due to his complexion. However, he felt a little embarrassed, but at the same time, he was delighted to receive such a compliment… especially from her. “Thank you,” he finally said with a smile. “I really do appreciate that.”

“You’re welcome. Any girl would be lucky enough to have you as their boyfriend.”

Brittany flirtatiously smiled at Myles. Then, they locked eyes. It was in that moment that they were willing to put aside anything that would stop them from giving in to their inhibitions. They slowly began to move in as if they were about to kiss, but suddenly, they heard footsteps approaching them, and they immediately broke their intimate gaze.

"Hey, babe," Daniel greeted as he walked up and kissed Brittany on the cheek.

"Hey!" Brittany said addressing Daniel, but a little disappointed that her moment with Myles was ruined. Then, she asked, "Where have you been?"

"I had to go to the bathroom," he answered. Then, he turned to Myles. "You have a pretty nice place in there, Myles. I mean, it's not as nice as my spot…"

"Daniel," Brittany said with a stern tone warning him that he was beginning to head down the wrong path.

"I'm just kidding," Daniel responded. "Look man, after what took place the last few days, our lives will never be back to normal. And because of everything that happened, we will be bonded together for the rest of our lives."

"Agreed," Myles stated. Then, he asked, "So… are we cool?"

Daniel hesitated for a moment. He looked at Brittany, and then, Brittany gave him a look, signifying to him what needed to happen next. Then, Daniel finally answered, "Yeah. We're cool."

Daniel held his hand out as Myles grabbed his hand, and they both shook in agreement that they were on good terms. "How about I whoop you in a game of one-on-one later?" Daniel challenged.

"You're on," Myles laughed.

Daniel laughed as well as he put his arm around Brittany, and they both walked away from Myles. Myles watched as the girl of his dreams was walking with someone else. However, without Daniel paying attention, Brittany turned her head and looked back at Myles as they locked eyes creating that connection of intimacy once again.

Meanwhile, back on the porch, Naomi and Jared were still talking and laughing.

"I still can't believe all of that happened," Naomi said.

"I know, right?" Jared added. "What's your dad saying about the school being repaired?"

"Everything should be back and running in the next few weeks. I can't believe I'm saying this, but I am so ready to being able to physically go back to school instead of homeschooling. Sheesh! You thought my dad was tough at school… try dealing with him in the house."

"I can only imagine."

"However, Daddy did say that there will be extra security added in order to protect us from any scary horsemen or demonic creatures trying to attack us," Naomi informed Jared.

"Well, let's just pray we won't see any of that ever again."

"I'm with you on that one."

Just as Naomi made her final statement, they looked up to see Deek walking up to them. She was wearing a black shirt, black jeans, and black boots; however, she now had little patches of scarlet sewn into her outfit in different areas. She was also wearing scarlet eye shadow to go along with her black mascara and lipstick.

"Hey, Deek!" Jared excitedly greeted. "You made it!"

"Yeah... I… um… I almost didn't," she admitted.

“Well, we’re glad you did,” Naomi warmly welcomed with a smile.

Deek smiled back as the aroma of freshly grilled turkey burgers and turkey dogs could be smelled across the yard. “Come on kids! The food is ready!” Mr. Taylor shouted as Mrs. Taylor placed the food on the table.

Deek, Jared, Naomi, Daniel, Brittany, and Myles joined Mr. and Mrs. Taylor around the table. “Myles, can you please say the blessing, son?” Mr. Taylor requested.

“Sure, Dad,” Myles answered. “Can everyone please bow your heads?”

Everyone bowed their heads and closed their eyes as they began to go into prayer.

“Dear Heavenly Father,” Myles prayed, “thank you so very much for this food that we are about to receive, and we ask that you please bless the hands that prepared it. We thank you for our lives, our health, the love and safety of our family and friends, and the opportunity for… new beginnings. Oh, and we ask that you please tell Michael that we said, ‘What’s up.’”

Deek, Jared, Naomi, Daniel, and Brittany smiled happily while Mr. Taylor had a confused look on his face.

He leaned over to his wife and whispered, "Who's Michael?"

"Shhhhhhhh!" Mrs. Taylor quietly responded instructing her husband to be quiet.

Myles continued, "And it's in Jesus' Name that we pray, Amen."

"Amen!" everyone happily repeated.

One by one, Myles, Jared, Naomi, Brittany, Daniel, and Deek, along with Mr. and Mrs. Taylor, each grabbed a plate and began to fix their plates. After they finished getting their food, they sat down together. While eating their delicious meal, they all talked and laughed and continued to enjoy fellowshipping with each other as the smoke from the grill travelled into the air and happiness and joy continued to fill the heavens.

However, unbeknownst to everyone down below, as the smoke filled the sky, Nefarious' face suddenly appeared amongst the smolder. "I… WILL… BE BACK!" Nefarious sinisterly cackled, and just as the smoke began to disappear, so did he. However, the potential peril of the wicked warning of his possible return continued to resonate in the sky trying to disturb the peace that surrounded and protected the atmosphere.

THE END

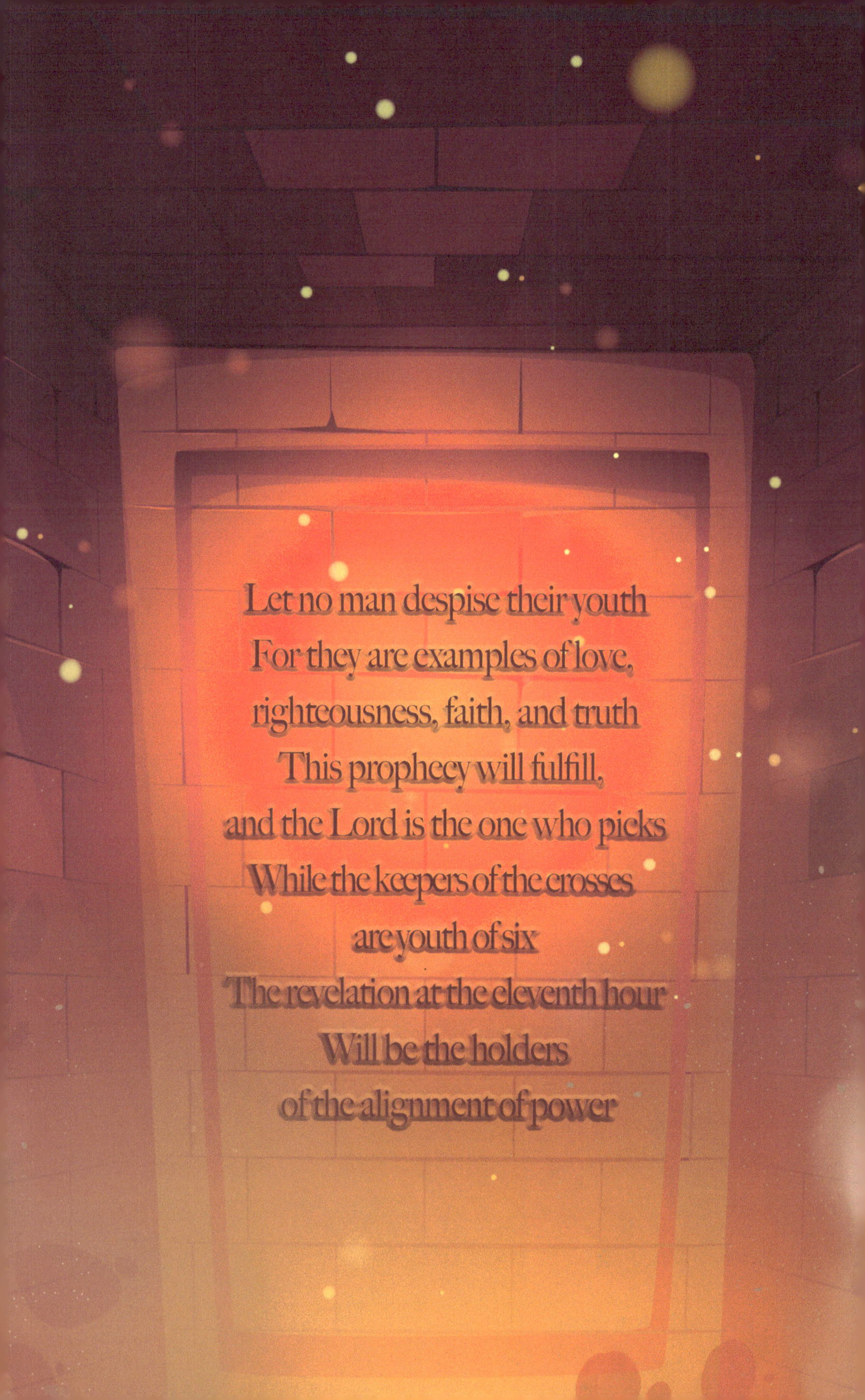

Let no man despise their youth
For they are examples of love,
righteousness, faith, and truth
This prophecy will fulfill,
and the Lord is the one who picks
While the keepers of the crosses
are youth of six
The revelation at the eleventh hour
Will be the holders
of the alignment of power

IT IS WRITTEN!

KARLTON T. CLAY has always loved to write. He began writing at a very young age. But it wasn't until his time at Davidson Fine Arts School in Augusta, GA that he began to get involved in production and wanting to use his gift of writing as his career. However, on March 18th, 2002, at the age of 16, Karlton was diagnosed with acute lymphoma leukemia; however, from this terrible life-altering experience, VICTORY PRODUCTIONS was born. Karlton graduated from Davidson Fine Arts School in 2004, and he graduated from Georgia State University in 2008 with a bachelor's degree in film and television production.

Under Victory Productions, Karlton has written, produced, and directed several theatre productions, short films, 15 series totaling 424 episodes, and 11 feature films which can be streamed on NBC's Peacock TV, FOX's Tubi, Sony's Crackle, and other streaming services. His content can also be viewed at **thevpntv.com**.

Karlton is also the author of a 4-part book series entitled *As The Earth Spins* and two poetry books: *Ebbs & Flows* (2020) and *Raw-N-UnKut* (2022) – both titles are also available as EPs under the moniker **KayCee Thee Poet** on all digital platforms.

Karlton is the son of Pastor Kenneth and Sonya Clay. He is the oldest of 6 children: Kendra, Karmen (Ashley DJ Scott), Kameron (Akeia), and his two heavenly sisters, Kimberly Monique and Kristina Miracle. Karlton is also the proud uncle of his two nephews, Kyler Terrell and Ashley Dante, and two nieces, Kimberly Alise and Peyton Elizabeth Kristina. He is also the happy dog-brother of the furry member of the family, Poochie.

In everything he does, Karlton hopes to remain true to who he is and be that beacon of hope that will inspire others to follow their dreams. His motto: Grow as you go, which is based off of his favorite scripture, "I can do all things through Christ who strengthens me." (Philippians 4:13)

CPSIA information can be obtained
at www.ICGtesting.com
Printed in the USA
JSHW072320070623
42878JS00001B/1
* 9 7 8 1 7 3 5 3 0 2 8 2 9 *